PETER CORRIS

THE DUNBAR CASE

ALLEN&UNWIN
SYDNEY • MELBOURNE • AUCKLAND • LONDON

First published in 2013

Copyright © Peter Corris 2013

Allen & Unwin
Sydney, Melbourne, Auckland, London

83 Alexander Street
Crows Nest NSW 2065
Australia
Phone: (61 2) 8425 0100
Email: info@allenandunwin.com
Web: www.allenandunwin.com

Cataloguing-in-Publication details are available
from the National Library of Australia
www.trove.nla.gov.au

ISBN 978 1 74331 751 8

Cover design by Emily O'Neill/Kirby Armstrong
Internal design by Emily O'Neill
Set in 12/17 pt pt Adobe Caslon by Midland Typesetters, Australia
Printed and bound in Australia by Griffin Press

This project has been assisted by the Australian Government through the Australia Council for the Arts, its arts funding and advisory body.

10 9 8 7 6 5 4 3

B000 000 011 8459

Praise for *The Dunbar Case*:

'. . . there's never, ever a dull moment and Corris keeps it moving in his lively, economical prose. Like the crime-meister that he is, Corris makes it all appear so easy.
Sue Turnbull *Sydney Morning Herald*

'A five-time winner of the Ned Kelly award for best crime novel, author and academic Corris deftly weaves together the strands of a busy plot before giving the whole skein a final breathtaking twist. But what lifts it out of the ordinary is his wry social commentary, keen insight into human nature and spare vernacular prose.'
Anne Partlon *Weekend Australian*

'Private eye tales always make good beach reading and few do it better than veteran Australian author Peter Corris . . . The pacing is brisk and Corris smoothly mixes interesting history with modern thrills. The story is engaging and Corris builds it to a taut, exciting climax.'
Jeff Popple *Canberra Times*

PETER CORRIS is known as the 'godfather' of Australian crime fiction through his Cliff Hardy detective stories. He has written in many other areas, including a co-authored autobiography of the late Professor Fred Hollows, a history of boxing in Australia, spy novels, historical novels and a collection of short stories about golf (see www.petercorris. net). In 2009, Peter Corris was awarded the Ned Kelly Award for Best Fiction by the Crime Writers Association of Australia. He is married to writer Jean Bedford and has lived in Sydney for most of his life. They have three daughters and five grandsons.

Peter Corris's thirty-eight Cliff Hardy books include *The Empty Beach*, *Master's Mates*, *The Coast Road*, *Saving Billie*, *The Undertow*, *Appeal Denied*, *The Big Score*, *Open File*, *Deep Water*, *Torn Apart*, *Follow the Money*, *Comeback* and *The Dunbar Case*.

For Stephen Wallace

Gloomy cliffs so worn and wasted, with the
washing of the waves,
Are ye not like giant tombstones round
those lonely ocean graves?

'Drowned at Sea', by Henry Kendall (1839–1882)

part one

1

I was sitting in Anton's on King, a restaurant in Newtown. French. I suppose there were Antons elsewhere but 'on King' is a popular tag and pretty well all Sydney diners would know from that where it was. Anton's wasn't the sort of place I usually ate at. Way too expensive. It had all the trimmings— the muted lighting, sound-absorbing walls and floor, white tablecloths, gleaming glass and silverware and attractive waitresses. I was enjoying the ambience because I knew I wouldn't be paying for it. My client, Henry Wakefield, had suggested—call it insisted on—the venue.

'Mr Hardy,' he'd said in rounded private school tones when he rang, 'Roberta Landy-Drake recommended you to me and I was pleased to find you online. My name is Wakefield, Henry Wakefield.'

'That was kind of Roberta,' I said. 'How can I help you, Mr Wakefield?'

'Initially, you can help by agreeing to lunch with me to discuss something.'

He proposed the day, the time and Anton's. I asked a few questions but he fended them off, saying that it was a confidential matter. It was a very different approach to what I'd become used to—the sad requests to trace missing teenagers, the low-paid serving of demands for court appearances, the surveillance of alleged stalkers, workplace bullies and sexual harassers. That kind of work brought in a more or less steady cash flow for a private detective, but did nothing for the sense of self-worth. Nor did the jobs I'd done for Roberta Landy-Drake—mostly keeping order at her upmarket but volatile parties—but they paid much better.

From time to time there were more interesting jobs and I remained ever hopeful. Wakefield had suggested we meet in two days; no great urgency then. Another unusual feature. I awaited his arrival with interest.

'A drink while you're waiting, sir?'

'Why not? A light beer, please.'

She named several brands and I picked the only one I was familiar with. I'd done a web check on Wakefield. He was a professor of history at the Independent University, an institution I knew nothing about so I had to check that out as well. Wakefield had degrees from a couple of American universities I'd never heard of, and the IU was a new outfit privately funded from corporate sources. It had a small campus in Newtown. From the photograph it seemed to consist of four three-storey terrace houses opposite a park two blocks east of King Street—just a short stroll for the prof to Anton's. The web page didn't say so, but from the elaborate coat of arms and the motto—'Knowledge is Power'—I got the feeling that the IU would charge pretty hefty fees. I was surprised that such a place would teach history at all, but I suppose there are lots of ways of teaching it.

I was early. I always am. I call it professional caution but it's really an anxiety, or maybe both. The beer arrived, very cold, in a beautiful glass. As someone who'd enjoyed a public school education and hadn't enjoyed a few years at university when it was free, I was critical of the way money dominated the sector now. I was prepared to dislike Professor Wakefield and settle for a free lunch. Jimmy Carter was wrong about that as about so many other things, particularly cardigan-wearing.

Wakefield came in precisely on time. The head-shot on the web page had flattered him a little, but he was impressively tall, with a good head of hair and a beard—both silver although he wasn't old. He was trim and looked to be a few years short of fifty. With the day sunny and mild, he wore a lightweight beige suit. He would. I was in a light linen jacket and drill trousers myself, but Wakefield wore a stylish light blue shirt and a silk tie, while I wore a T-shirt. Clean, though.

The restaurant was filling up and Wakefield nodded to a few fellow eaters and sketched an almost bow to the waitress in charge as he advanced towards my table. No big trick to that—my mug shot was on my web page, too. Body language is very important. If you stay seated at a meeting, a natural bully or dominant type will loom over you as he extends his hand. An egalitarian will take his seat first. Wakefield hesitated just long enough to make me feel he inclined towards option one, before dropping into his chair and sticking his hand out across the snowy surface.

'Henry Wakefield.'

'Cliff Hardy, Professor. Pleased to meet you.'

'Henry, please.'

A waitress was hovering and Wakefield pointed to my half-full glass. 'The same for me, please, and don't bother about the menu.'

He undid the top button of his shirt and slid his tie knot down. 'Good place, this.'

I nodded. Was his accent now a shade closer to mine? Possibly.

'I recommend the whitebait for starters and the swordfish for a main,' Wakefield said. 'Unless you'd care to study the menu.'

'That'll do me,' I said.

His beer arrived and he held the waitress by the arm. 'Wine?'

'Sure.'

'A bottle of that New Zealand riesling I like, please, Suzie.'

'Yes, Professor.'

He gave our order to another waitress without touching her and drank half of his beer in a couple of manly gulps. 'I gather you like to get straight down to business.'

'That's right, but you're paying so you can call the shots.'

He drained his glass. 'Have you ever heard of the wreck of the *Dunbar*?'

'I don't think so.'

'A luxury passenger vessel. In August 1857 she was wrecked when trying to enter Sydney Harbour—'

'I'm with you now. There's a monument down the way in St Stephen's cemetery.'

He didn't like being interrupted. The wine arrived and he was too irritated to be polite to Suzie. He tasted it and nodded. 'Good. Thanks. Yes, that's right. Do you know the details?'

I shook my head. He was a prospective client and there was no point in annoying him further. Anyway, I didn't know the details. I'd just had a passing look at the monument when wandering one day in the cemetery with my daughter Megan and grandson Ben. Megan lived a stone's throw away.

'The *Dunbar* was driven onto the rocks and she was holed and sank quickly. A storm was raging. As things stand, no one knows why the captain, who was very experienced in those waters, attempted the entry, given the conditions. One hundred and twenty-one people, passengers and crew, were drowned. There was, so the story goes, one survivor.'

The whitebait appeared and we dug in. Wakefield seemed

to be torn between giving his full attention to the food and going on with his story. The food won and there was no way he'd talk with his mouth full. He poured the wine. The fish was crisp and delicious, so was the wine. We both used pieces of bread to wipe our plates.

He looked at me, his clear grey eyes keen and penetrating under trimmed white eyebrows. 'You've registered something in what I've said.'

'Yeah, you implied that there's more to the story than—'

His turn to interrupt. 'Yes, much more. Mind you, the story is dramatic enough as it is—tremendous loss of life, greatest maritime disaster ever, bodies washing up on the beaches for days, a navigational mystery and one survivor.'

He had my attention and I found I was able to remember something about the monument in the cemetery. It was a fenced-in white structure, something between a grave and a memorial stone. The writing had been partly obliterated by time and the weather. 'Wasn't there something about another ship?'

'You're thinking of the mass grave. Yes, the *Catherine Adamson*. That doesn't matter.'

The entrée plates were whisked away to be replaced by the swordfish with baby carrots, snow peas and new potatoes. We both accepted ground pepper. It was eating time again and we started. The words 'mass grave' had triggered more memories—the remains of people drowned from two ships were interred but, according to Wakefield, only those from the *Dunbar* mattered. Single-minded and not long on compassion. Well, perhaps that's the way you have to be to become a professor at a corporate university.

The restaurant was about two-thirds full, a good crowd for a Wednesday lunch and easy enough for the staff to handle. I sensed that Wakefield was keen to go on with his story but the food and wine deserved attention. A few pauses, however, were in order and during them he got on with it.

He said that a good many of the sixty-three passengers on the *Dunbar* were Sydney residents returning from a trip to England and there were Sydneysiders among the fifty-eight crew. This meant that family members were involved in identifying bodies or trying to find them. The city went into mourning, shops and banks closed and churches were full. Twenty thousand people watched the funeral procession.

'A seaman with the uninteresting name of James Johnson was apparently thrown from the deck onto the rocks when the ship struck. He clung on there through the night and was spotted the next day and hauled up.'

'Where was this, exactly?'

Wakefield dealt with a chunk of fish before answering. 'Off South Head; the fool of a captain apparently thought he was approaching North Head and gave the wrong order.'

There didn't seem to be anything to say so I just nodded and got on with my meal. A few years back I'd had some dealings with an academic historian who became impassioned about his subject when there looked to be a chance of latching on to something new. Wakefield didn't give off that kind of vibe, but from the way he settled down to cleaning his plate I sensed that he was working up to something important even if it didn't seem to excite him overmuch.

We both sat back with empty plates and the last of the wine in our glasses.

'The *Dunbar* story has been pretty well cut and dried for a long time,' Wakefield said. 'The wreck was only nine metres down and they located it early on. Divers retrieved various things in the 1960s. There's an exhibition of relics in the Maritime Museum—worth a look, but only just—and the grave in the cemetery is a Newtown tourist feature. Do you want dessert or coffee?'

'Coffee, please, but what I really want is for you to give me some idea of the relevance of all this to me. It's very interesting but . . .'

'You're right, I've let myself get off track. I understand you were in the army.'

'A long time ago.'

'Where, if I may ask?'

'Here and there.'

'And you were a boxer?'

'Amateur.'

'And you were in gaol?'

'Again, a while back. Where is this heading?'

'I need someone who's resourceful, discreet and experienced at dealing with the rougher elements in society.'

'To do what?'

'To find someone and persuade them to give something up for a fair price.'

'There's no such thing as a fair price, Professor, there's—'

'Henry.'

'—only a matter of what it's worth to whoever's selling and whoever's buying.'

He drained his glass and beamed—the first full-blown emotional reaction I'd seen from him. 'That's splendid, worthy of some of my colleagues in the Business School. Very pithy. You said coffee. Long black?'

I nodded. He ordered two from the waiter, who cleared the table. He leaned forward as if wary about being overheard, although the space between the tables and the buzz of sound in the place made our conversation private.

'There was another survivor,' he said.

2

Wakefield reached into the pocket of his jacket, pulled out a fat wallet and selected a card which he passed over to me as the long blacks arrived. The card had the university's embossed coat of arms and motto and carried his name and titles, including 'Director of the Center for Australian Historical Revision'.

I read the card, sipped the coffee. 'C-e-n-t-e-r?'

He shrugged. 'For the Americans. We have a fresh approach that appeals to our corporate supporters here and abroad. A determination to take an entirely new look at the major signposts in this country's history.'

'The *Dunbar*'s a major signpost?'

'Perhaps not, but it offers a chance to put the centre on the map because I believe there was another survivor and a manuscript that offers a different version of events. If I can secure it, quite apart from its not insignificant monetary value, it'd lend credibility to the enterprise I've staked my career on. I make no bones about that. I was lucky to get this appointment and I'll only be able to hold it if I show results. The backers, shall we call them, are impatient people.'

'You need a win?'

'I do. And I need your help.'

It was a tricky moment. I hoped he wasn't one of those revisionists who wanted to say that only a few Aborigines were killed on the frontiers, that the White Australia policy never existed and that Australia was in danger of German invasion in 1914. But my newly revived agency wasn't doing too well in a year of local disasters like the Christchurch earthquake, the floods and the demolition of the ALP in the recent state election, and I couldn't afford to turn down work from someone with a wallet that size. I had office rent and a six-figure mortgage to cover. And, as a sucker for Sydney history, I found the story interesting.

'I'm listening, Henry,' I said.

He finished his coffee. The wallet was still on the table and he took out a credit card. 'Let's set the scene,' he said, 'a post-prandial stroll to the cemetery.'

It was late in March, a month when Sydney can decide it's time for winter to take a grip or, like that day, can bring on spring early. We joined the young and the old, the freaks and the suits, walking along King Street past the boutiques and eateries and turned down Church Street.

'A bit like Lower Manhattan,' Wakefield said as he stepped over a milk crate.

'Spent a bit of time there, have you?'

'Mmm. Some.'

'At Columbia?'

He glanced sharply at me. 'No, I was upstate mostly.'

We reached the church grounds and crunched down the path past the Moreton Bay figs, shrubs and flowers I couldn't identify, and weathered headstones.

'This is all in a disgraceful state,' Wakefield said.

'I don't know, it's got an authentic feel, sort of restful, as if no one's bothering them and never will.'

He grunted. The church was quiet; we left the path and moved into the graveyard area proper where the roots of the trees pushed up and threatened to trip you and the grass grew in tussocks around the headstones and fenced graves. I had only the vaguest memory of where the monument was but Wakefield went straight to where it stood, white and imposing, inside a rusted iron fence, in pride of place in the middle of a recess in the east wall of the cemetery.

The dark lettering on the monument had suffered some attrition at the edges but most of it had remained clear enough: WITHIN THIS TOMB WERE DEPOSITED BY DIRECTION OF THE GOVERNMENT OF NEW SOUTH WALES SUCH REMAINS AS COULD BE DISCOVERED OF THE PASSENGERS AND CREW

WHO PERISHED IN THE SHIPS 'DUNBAR' AND 'CATHERINE'. THE FORMER OF WHICH WAS DRIVEN ASHORE AND FOUNDERED WHEN APPROACHING THE ENTRANCE TO PORT JACKSON ON THE NIGHT OF THE 20TH OF AUGUST THE LATTER ON ENTERING THIS PORT ON THE MORNING OF THE 24TH OF OCTOBER.

AD 1857 was engraved at the base of the tomb.

A mass grave is a sad thing, it seems to me, but if Wakefield had entertained such feelings he'd got over them.

'Quite a few of the victims, those they could identify, are buried here,' he said, 'and a couple in this spot, but you'd be hard put to read the headstones now, apart from that one.'

He pointed to a well-preserved white headstone for John Steane, a naval officer who'd lost his life when the *Dunbar* went down.

'A hundred and fifty-odd years is a long time,' I said.

Wakefield took care not to brush against the fence. 'You're thinking it's a long time-lapse to be tracking something down.'

I shrugged. 'It's what, five generations?'

'Fewer in this case; four in fact. It's a great-grandson of the survivor I'm interested in. That's not a very long stretch as these things go. Some of the people claiming Aboriginal or convict ancestry have to push back a lot further than that.'

'I know,' I said. 'My sister found a convict ancestor for us way back. She was a London prostitute.'

'Colourful,' Wakefield said, moving away from the

monument. 'As you may or may not know, we academics get our postgraduate students to do some of our research. They earn their degrees and go on to bigger and better things and ...'

'You write your books. I've heard of it.'

We moved between the headstones back to the path.

'You object?'

'No. I suppose it's subject to abuse, but what isn't?'

'Just so. I was able to discover a reliable list of the passengers aboard the *Dunbar*. That took time and effort, let me tell you. There were many uncertainties. I set some students to tracing descendants of the victims—direct descendants. One of them found a record of a child born to one of the passengers in 1883. You see the implication of that date?'

'Yeah, if it's not a clerical error.'

'It isn't. You're interested?'

'Maybe.'

'Fair enough. What I propose is this—I show you the fruits of my research so far, on an understanding of complete confidentiality, and the ... direction in which it's heading and, if you're still interested, we come to an arrangement.'

I thought he might be going to invite me back to the university but he didn't. When I said I was in the car park behind the supermarket we stopped there and shook hands. He asked for my card and I gave it to him. He said he'd email me a document and that I should read it and get back to him with my thoughts. I thanked him for the lunch and watched him stride away—straight-backed, head up, one of the winners.

Or was he? I decided I had a fair bit of checking to do on him, on the university and on the *Dunbar* before I took this assignment. It might amount to no more than a good, a very good, lunch.

I went to my office in Pyrmont, paid a few bills, wrote the dates due on a couple of others and placed them where they'd stare at me. The office has no views to speak of, which is how I like it. My previous offices, in Darlinghurst and Newtown, carried a lot of memories, of clients good and bad, encounters pleasant and unpleasant, so that sometimes I could sit there reliving the experiences. A bad habit and it didn't operate here where I hadn't been very long and the memories were too recent to dwell upon.

I Googled the *Dunbar* and was soon immersed in details of the ship and its unhappy fate. While the whole episode didn't have the dimensions of the *Titanic* disaster, the ship was luxurious for its time, with some very smart cabins, and it had been custom-built as a fast ship to compete with American vessels in the era of the gold rushes. The crew was said to be first class and the captain, James Green, was a veteran of eight previous voyages to Sydney.

Wakefield's uncharitable account of Green's navigational error was more or less accurate. The *Dunbar* slammed broadside into the cliffs between the Gap and the Macquarie

Lighthouse, which wasn't completely effective in bad weather, and her solid construction of British oak and Indian teak couldn't save her.

I read through the accounts of the inquiries and the exoneration of Green that attributed the tragedy to the extreme weather, and James Johnson's testimony that seemed to have, understandably, a shell-shocked quality to it. Survivors carry a burden of guilt no matter how innocent they are, and Johnson was defensive and anxious to withdraw from the limelight. He later distinguished himself by brave actions in connection with another wrecked vessel and, interestingly, accounts of this carried a flavour of rehabilitation, as if the poor bugger had lived something down. I'd been there.

I printed out a few pages and sat back from this pretty superficial research thinking how unfair history could be. I had to admit to being very interested, even intrigued. Wakefield's claim to be able to track another survivor and another account of events was as compelling as a treasure island map.

I didn't learn much more about Wakefield from the web. He'd written a few articles in minor journals and a book for a small Californian publisher on Australians in the California gold rush. You could pick it up very cheap on Amazon.

There was no email from Wakefield by late in the afternoon so I did my usual workout at the Redgum Gym in Leichhardt.

I'd had a quadruple bypass a few years before and had to take various medications at various times under different conditions that annoyed me and made me feel fragile. I tended to work too hard in the gym to prove I wasn't.

Then I paid Megan and Ben a visit. Megan was working on her laptop while keeping an eye on Ben, who was watching a DVD of *The Gruffalo*. I gave him a gingerbread man and he gave me a thumbs-up without taking his eyes off the screen.

'He particularly likes the scary bits,' she said. 'Should I be worried?'

'I liked Mr Hyde better than Dr Jekyll,' I said.

'Look where it got you. But I have to say, Cliff, you're more like yourself today than you have been lately.'

'What d'you mean?'

'You've looked bored, now you look almost excited. Something on your plate? Tell me you're not going undercover for ICAC.'

I laughed and told her about Wakefield. She remembered the tomb in the cemetery and the wording 'such remains as could be discovered . . .' The mass grave had had the same effect on her as me. They'd had to do something similar in Christchurch after the earthquake and even more extensively in Japan after the earthquake and tsunami.

Megan shut down the laptop. 'Is he fair dinkum?'

'I don't know. He's from Queensland, although you wouldn't know it from his accent. He's got these degrees from little US colleges and a few publications in not very impressive places. I don't think you'd want Ben to go to the Independent University. It's mostly online stuff and the thrust is for personal achievement and organisational management. Apparently there's a lot to learn about the dynamics between those two.'

'I bet. Still, it's got you in and it'll pay.'

'It might. How's Hank?'

Hank Bachelor was Megan's partner and Ben's father. He'd given his genes to the boy. Hank stood 190 centimetres and when they measured Ben at two years of age and doubled the figure, a formula which is supposed to give you the fully grown height of a child, he clocked in at 195. Hank had worked for me in the past and now he was on his own, specialising in surveillance equipment.

'He's fine,' Megan said. 'Busy, but he misses the street stuff he used to do with you.'

'There's not much of it around these days.'

'You usually manage to find some. Take care of yourself, Cliff, you're not . . .'

'As young as I look. I know.'

I kissed her and said goodbye to Ben, who gave me a double thumbs-up.

The email was there when I got to my home computer in the morning. I couldn't open the attachment. An hour later Wakefield rang.

'You got my email?'

'Yes, I can't open the attachment.'

'Of course not. You need a password.'

'I tried *Dunbar* just for fun.'

He chuckled. 'The password is Twizell.' He spelled the word. 'Call me when you've read what I've written.'

I opened the attachment. It had no heading and ran to twenty pages. Wakefield's prose was functional rather than elegant:

Research has revealed that William Dalgarno Twizell may have survived the wreck on the *Dunbar*. Twizell was born in South Shields, Durham, 17/8/1808. A master mariner, who had captained vessels in the British merchant marine for twenty years, he was a skilled navigator who had also worked as a pilot in various ports around the world as a break from his captaincy responsibilities. He was fit, single and had taken passage on the *Dunbar* to Australia, where he had been several times before, to take up the command of a coastal trading vessel. He had no family connections in Australia. His body was not discovered after the wreck.

The document went on to say that a birth certificate had been discovered registering the birth of a Robert Dalgarno Twizell in Newcastle on 3 March 1883. The mother, Catharine Lucy Tanner, had registered the birth and the father's name was given as William Dalgarno Twizell with the birth date of

17 August 1808; the birthplace was Durham, England. An entry on the certificate noted that the father was deceased.

Wakefield, or his students, had traced Robert Twizell, who appeared to have been a man of some means, the owner of a couple of ships and himself an experienced mariner. Robert Twizell married late and fathered a son and a daughter. The son, born in 1925, also Robert, did not prosper. He had a spotty criminal record as a youth, joined the 2nd AIF in 1944, was invalided out in 1945 and fought a long battle with the authorities over his entitlement to a serviceman's pension. The matter was unresolved when he died of lung cancer in 1988.

I made some notes as I read, forgetting that I could print out the whole thing. Old habits die hard. Despite his claimed service disabilities—damage to hearing and eyesight and malaria contracted during his brief time in the catering corps in New Guinea—Twizell married and had three sons, all born close together in the early 1970s. One son, Robin, was drowned off Newcastle beach in 1980; another, Hunter, was killed in a car accident when driving drunk after his father's funeral in 1988. The surviving son, John Dalgarno Twizell, was in gaol.

3

I rang the university when I'd finished reading and asked for Professor Wakefield in the History Department.

'History? Oh, that'd be Human Studies, I suppose,' the switchboard operator said. 'I'll put you through.'

'Wakefield.'

'This is Hardy.'

'Good. Well?'

'It's compelling.'

'I imagine you have questions.'

'A few. No death certificate for William Twizell, I take it?'

'No. He must have used another name.'

'Why would he do that?'

'In your experience, why do people adopt other names?'

'Because they have something to hide.'

'Exactly. What you've read is just an outline. There's a good deal more to tell you that I'm not prepared to commit to writing just at the moment. We should meet again and I'll tell you more. Then we can get things on a business footing. I see you have an office in Pyrmont.'

'That's right.'

'Not far from the Maritime Museum where the *Dunbar* exhibit is. I propose that we meet there.'

'You're assuming . . . ?'

'I'm assuming that you want me to sign a contract, agree to your terms, pay you a retainer, and enlist your help on this fascinating project.'

I didn't like him or his manner but the curiosity bug had bitten me. I said that I'd hold off until he'd told me a bit more and I'd bring a contract with me.

'That's reasonable,' he said.

We agreed to meet at the Maritime Museum at 2pm.

He tried for a light touch. 'There's no admission fee. You can't claim it as an expense.'

'I might decide to make the deal retrospective to the beginning of our meeting yesterday. Charge you for the time and research.'

'Touché,' he said.

I remember when Darling Harbour was a derelict jumble of disused goods lines, sagging sheds and machinery rusted beyond recognition. They got to work in the late '80s and transformed it into the people-friendly precinct it is now.

It's money-friendly too, of course. A flat white'll set you back four bucks and what it costs to hire one of the display areas or conference set-ups I don't like to think. But the layout, with the paved walkways, the water features and grassy bits, is tasteful and calming, a big plus in a modern city.

I enjoyed the walk from Pyrmont and the feeling that, although the city was humming around me, I could access some tranquillity with a little exercise. The Maritime Museum was one of those modern light and airy structures that looked as if they could float away but was actually all solid concrete, glass and steel.

Wakefield, in a grey suit more appropriate to the duller day, was standing outside the museum talking on his mobile phone. He raised a hand in greeting and I hung back until he'd finished. Some people are happy to carry on a mobile phone and a live conversation at the same time or to text while they're talking to you. Not me.

He slid the phone into his pocket and patted himself to make sure it hadn't disturbed the line of the jacket.

'Good afternoon, Cliff. I hope we're on those terms now.'

'Henry.' We shook hands.

'Fine structure, isn't it?' He gestured at the museum.

'It looks right for what it is.'

'True. Let's go inside and I'll show you what they've got on the ship.'

We were given stick-on visitor tags and went up a series of ramps into the heart of the building.

'It's part of the Age of Sail section,' Wakefield said. His tone was condescending. 'Nicely done, I'd say.'

He conducted me unerringly through a succession of rooms and passages with muted light and stopped in front of a large glass showcase. The exhibit contained a sizeable painting of the vessel in full sail and a collection of items brought up from the wreck—coins, buttons, bottles, a watch, rings.

'The water's turbulent at that spot,' Wakefield said. 'A great deal of the material would have been carried away immediately. The bottom is sandy and sand shifts. This is all the divers retrieved.'

I leaned close to the glass. 'It's effective, I'd say. It's modest, but I reckon it captures the sadness of the event.'

'Yes, I suppose so.'

I took a good look at the painting. 'It was a beautiful ship.'

'Yes it was and it cost a lot to travel in the best cabins. There were some wealthy people aboard. That's an important part of the story. Let's get on with things.'

We retraced our steps and walked to the nearest café. Wakefield asked to see my contract. He looked through it quickly and took out a silver pen and a chequebook.

'Very professional,' he said.

'Hold on. You were going to fill me in some more before we signed up.'

'I've never met anyone so reluctant to get his hands on serious money. Okay, to pick up from where we left off—a man with something to hide and wealthy people aboard the ship.'

'Go on.'

'One of the passengers was a man named Daniel Abrahams. A Jew, of course, he was born in America and had spent some time in South Africa. I can't begin to tell you how difficult it has been to trace his story through various sources but the upshot is this—he found diamonds in South Africa about ten years before anyone else. He'd been hired to prospect for them by one of the companies that eventually established the huge diamond mines in that country, but he . . . broke faith with them. He failed to report his discovery, took a large cache of diamonds and fled to England.'

'Bloody diamonds,' I said.

'Excuse me?'

'They've caused more trouble in the world than they're worth.'

'If you say so. The point is, Abrahams seems to have thought he was in danger in England and he took a ship to Australia.'

I'd ordered coffee. Wakefield ignored it when it arrived and went on with his story.

'Abrahams was aboard the *Dunbar* with a fortune in diamonds in his possession. He was in one of the premium cabins and Twizell was right there beside him. Both were single; they would have hobnobbed.'

I drank some coffee. 'I feel you're stretching things a bit.'

'Not so. Almost everything I've said is documented.'

'Almost.'

'Just listen. Twizell's son owned three ships. How did he acquire them?'

'You tell me.'

'From his father, who bought them on the proceeds of selling Daniel Abraham's diamonds.'

'A fifty-year-old man swam ashore when the waves were smashing the boat to bits?'

'No. He left the ship at Bega when she offloaded a sick passenger. I believe that was Twizell.'

'There was an inquiry, wasn't there? Was this mentioned?'

'Who was there to mention it?'

'The survivor.'

'He wasn't asked.'

'People at Bega.'

'Ah, there you have it. An obscure report in a local news-paper about a sick passenger being transferred to a whaling vessel at the mouth of the bay.'

'You're drawing a very long bow.'

'I'd agree with you but for one thing.'

'That is?'

'At one point along the line in this tale a person who was in a position to know what happened wrote it all down. No, I shouldn't say that—is alleged to have written most of it down.'

When someone backtracks and dilutes a story in that

way it can be because they know they're on shaky ground and don't want to have to provide much more substance, or because they're being honest and trying to tell it like it is. With Wakefield, it was hard to judge.

'You've made a lot of assumptions and the documentation's pretty flimsy,' I said. 'I don't trust newspapers to do much beyond getting the date right.'

'I agree with you, but in this period such things are all we have. A good deal of accepted history is built on nothing much stronger.'

He was getting close to his chosen field of revisionary history and I didn't want to get into that. I was sure he could out-fence me there with examples and evidence.

'What exactly do you have in mind for me to do?'

'Just this—talk to John Twizell in Bathurst gaol. Ask him certain questions and report back on what he says.'

Put like that, what could I do? We signed the contract and Wakefield wrote me a cheque for a retainer that would keep the wolves from my door for the better part of a month. Generally speaking, these days I prefer a direct deposit into my working account, but with the chequebook and a silver pen in his hand I didn't feel like objecting. He signed with a flourish and handed the cheque to me. In the old days you could arrange to have cheques cleared instantly by paying a fee. Not any more.

'A question. If you're planning to write a book about this, wouldn't it be better for you to interview Twizell yourself?

I mean, wouldn't it add flavour? You'd be the investigator as well as the researcher. Save you money, too.'

He shook his head. 'Look at me, the modern, corporate, funded academic. I'd be out of my depth with someone like Twizell and likely to antagonise him. I'm assuming you know people in the . . . custodial industry—prison and parole officers, lawyers and the like?'

Custodial industry, I thought. Well, I guess that's what it is, more or less.

I nodded, folded the cheque and slipped it into my wallet. 'What's he in for?'

Putting the chequebook and pen away he looked slightly uncomfortable. 'Oh, didn't I say? He's serving a sentence for assault with a deadly weapon.'

4

I couldn't remember reading or hearing about Twizell, but a few years back I'd spent ten months in the US and in my delicensed period I didn't pay too much attention to what was happening on the dark side. With the *Sydney Morning Herald* online at the State Library it wasn't hard to catch up.

Four years earlier, when I was helping a friend prepare for championship fights in America, Twizell had been convicted of assaulting his lover, Kristine Tanner, in Newcastle. Drugs were involved and there was a fair degree of provocation. He was sentenced to seven years with five to serve before becoming eligible for parole. It was a sordid, run-of-the-mill case that hadn't attracted much media attention. The *Herald*'s reports were spare and there were few photographs. Twizell, thirty-nine, was a stocky individual with a shaved head and a belligerent stare; Kristine Tanner, thirty at the time of the attack, had been hospitalised for several months and had undergone extensive reconstructive surgery.

I printed out a couple of the reports and underlined some names. Twizell had been represented by Courtenay Braithwaite, who I didn't know but I was sure my solicitor, Viv Garner, would. One of the police officers giving testimony was Detective Inspector Kevin Rush, who I had met under not very friendly circumstances some time in the past. I also underlined the name Tanner without quite knowing why. I was punching in Viv's number when it came to me— Tanner was the name of the woman who'd registered the child Wakefield believed to be William Dalgarno Twizell's son. Well, it was a common enough name. I had a feeling there was something more to the name than that but I couldn't put my finger on it.

Viv knew Braithwaite.

'Is he any good?' I asked.

'Fair to middling.'

'Busy?'

'He's getting on like the rest of us. I shouldn't think so. Loves a drink.'

'Like the rest of us.'

'Speak for yourself. I'm off it.'

'If it doesn't make you live longer at least it'll feel like it.'

'He can be fun,' Viv said. He undertook to ring Braithwaite, vouching for me. I gave it a few hours and rang his chambers.

I was put through to him. He said he'd been glad to hear from Viv and asked how he could help.

'You represented John Twizell.'

I heard a wheezy sigh. 'I did. Not one of my successes.'

'I have a client who has an interest in him.'

'That's understandable; he's an interesting character in his way. What's the nature of the interest?'

I wasn't prepared to tell him much until I'd sized him up. 'Perhaps we could meet?'

He agreed, named a wine bar in Castlereagh Street and suggested five o'clock. Early for knock-off time. Looked as if he wasn't busy.

The Cellar Bar was one of those below-ground joints that enjoy popularity for a while before jaded, fickle drinkers move on to somewhere else. As the name implied it had a theme defined by low beams, wooden barrels and a flagstoned floor. Drinkers could sit at tables or on benches if they wanted to feel especially authentic. The lighting was soft but adequate to see what you were drinking, and there was muted piano music playing. At 5.05pm there were only three customers—a young woman and her rather older companion, and a man on his own with a glass in front of him and a newspaper open at the racing page.

I approached him. 'Mr Braithwaite?'

He looked up. He bore more than a passing resemblance

to the late Lionel Murphy—thinning grey hair, bags below the eyes, jowls and a nose that glowed like a stoplight.

'You'd be Cliff Hardy,' he said, 'the notorious private detective. I'm delighted to meet you. Can't understand why it's taken so long.'

He half rose and we shook hands. I'd had a lot of time for Lionel Murphy, who I'd met once or twice, not least because I had benefited from his no-fault divorce law, and I was prepared to like his look-alike.

'Don't sit down.' He drained his glass and held it towards me. 'Mine's a double brandy and soda.'

I went to the bar and bought his drink and a glass of red for me. Braithwaite was putting the paper in his briefcase when I got back to his table.

'You're a punter?' I said.

He took a pull on the drink and shook his head. 'Cheers. No, part-owner. Foolish, but it's an interest in my declining years. You're bearing up well after all the slings and arrows I've heard about.'

'Just about,' I said. 'I'd like to have a talk about John Twizell.'

'You realise I'm only talking to you because I'm interested in someone with your reputation and because Viv Garner says you can be trusted and I trust his judgement.'

There was nothing to say to that so I just drank some wine.

'Anyone else coming to me with an interest in Johnnie and I'd ring the police straight away.'

I'd been getting ready to relax into some kind of cautious but more or less cordial interchange, but this made me sit up straight. 'Why's that?'

'Outside of prison, Johnnie Twizell could count the days of his survival on one hand. Inside, he's doing well to last this long.'

'Please explain.'

'You've heard of Jobe Tanner, surely?'

I had, and that was the other reason the name had caught my eye in Wakefield's text. Tanner was a high-level Newcastle crime figure. A fingers-in-every-pie type who kept the really dirty stuff at arm's length while profiting from it. He'd been called before two royal commissions and had been charged a few times for conspiracy and other difficult-to-prove offences but acquitted. Witness intimidation was second nature to him. Braithwaite saw me processing the name and nodded.

'Kristie Tanner is his daughter. He swore to kill Twizell.'

'That seems extreme. He didn't kill the woman.'

'No, but he damaged her very severely. Her injuries were so bad that I succeeded in getting the judge to withhold the photographs from the jury. Prejudicial. It was about the only success I had in the matter. Jobe Tanner has the means to do it, particularly in the persons of two very nasty sons.'

It was a fair bet that Wakefield knew this and took it as a reason to hire someone with the right experience to approach Twizell. Megan was right: I seemed to find trouble without having to look for it. But I'd taken Wakefield's money and I needed it.

'You'd advise me to steer clear of Twizell,' I said.

'Absolutely, but I know from the look of you and your reputation that you won't. You'd better tell me what your interest is. I owe Viv Garner a favour or two and I might be able to suggest a way to keep you out of Tanner's clutches.'

He finished his drink and pushed the glass towards me. 'Listening's hard work and you'd better have another while you consider how much to tell me.'

He was a shrewd old bird and I liked him. I got the drinks and some nuts and settled down to give him a severely edited version of the story, preserving as many of Wakefield's confidences as I could. He listened closely, sipping his drink and nibbling nuts, seemingly unaffected by three double brandies.

'I'm not surprised that Johnnie Twizell has some interesting antecedents,' Braithwaite said when I'd finished. 'He's pretty much wasted his life with drugs and gambling and women but he's a man you feel could have done something better.'

'I know what you mean; unlike a lot of people you feel have got further than they should have. Politicians in particular.'

He laughed, setting up a wheezing coughing fit that turned his face purple. He pulled out a Ventolin inhaler and gave himself a few puffs.

'And judges,' he said when he'd got his breath back. He laughed again but suppressed it so that only a few slight coughs resulted. 'I don't suppose you can be more specific about this information your client is seeking.'

I shook my head. 'He's playing it very close to his chest. When I confirm that I can see Twizell he's going to text me a set of questions. From what I know it's about something written—a letter maybe, a diary or journal, a confession.'

'Intriguing. What's in it for Johnnie?'

'Money, possibly.'

'He'd appreciate that.'

'You like him?'

'I wouldn't say that. He has charm. He's amusing. Do you know what someone in his position needs above all? What we all need, come to that?'

'Tell me.'

'Something to look forward to. I must say I haven't got it. Do you have it, Mr Hardy?'

'I'd have to think about that.'

'Bad sign. Anyway, I'm on record as Johnnie's legal chap and I can recommend a visit for you as my representative.'

'Thank you.'

'Only snag is that I imagine the Tanners have a watching brief on Johnnie's visitors. You'll have to be careful.'

'I can manage that. Another drink?'

'No, three's my limit. I'll just sit on this one and contemplate mankind's folly.'

'Good name for a horse.'

He raised his old man's thick, snaggled eyebrows. 'Don't make me laugh. You saw what it did to me.'

The next day Braithwaite's secretary emailed me that an appointment had been made for me to visit Twizell in two days. A letter from the lawyer giving me his authority was attached.

I called Wakefield to report on my progress.

'I knew you were the man for the job,' he said.

'But you didn't tell me Twizell had savagely assaulted a female member of a notorious crime family. What else haven't you told me?'

'Nothing. Let's not get off on the wrong foot. When are you going to Bathurst?'

'Tomorrow, driving.'

'Call me when you arrive. I'll text the questions I want you to ask.'

I wasn't happy about it; I felt manipulated, but that was nothing new in the business I was in. The thing to do is to be aware of it and be prepared to manipulate back.

I'd got into the habit of letting Megan know when I was going to be out of town. She'd go to my house and collect the mail and sometimes she'd take Ben over to play there as a change from the flat. She needed to know that the coast was clear for that. She said she liked to be sure I didn't have a woman installed or visiting, but it had been a while since that had happened.

I hadn't expected grandfatherhood to affect me the way it did. I felt enormous relief when Megan's baby arrived safely and I thought that'd likely be the strongest emotion

I'd feel. Wrong. The first time I held Ben I felt something quite different. Perhaps because I'd missed out on Megan's babyhood I felt it more strongly than most grandfathers—a sense of the thread of life continuing.

That feeling eased off, of course, but a powerful sense of protectiveness and interest in the boy's development remained. I didn't go overboard. I did an occasional baby-sit and I installed a folding cot in my spare room. A few kids' books on the shelves down at his level and some plastic plates and eating gear.

'Bathurst?' Megan said when I phoned her. 'Never been there. Didn't they have some trouble about water a while back?'

'Yeah, I think they held a vote on whether to recycle sewage.'

'How did it go?'

'I think the nos won it.'

'That'd be right. Well, take care, Cliff. How long'll you be away?'

'Don't know.'

'That'd be right, too. Should be nice out there at this time of year. Bit bracing perhaps. Be sure to take all your pills with you.'

41

5

Town planners and social engineers lament that our population is concentrated in the capital cities of each state. They say the maximum functional size of a city is about two million and it's crazy that Sydney has five million plus people while Bathurst, only a couple of hundred kilometres away, has barely thirty thousand. It's different in America and better, they say, where regional cities help to spread the population out. They're probably right but it's a bit late now to make that change.

I was looking forward to the drive. Like most Sydneysiders, I don't want to live west of the Blue Mountains, but I like to visit. It can be cold out there so I packed some warm clothes in a bag, a bottle of Haig scotch and a carton of Camel cigarettes. I'd stopped smoking longer ago than I could remember, but, in my experience, many prisoners still smoked and wanted the hardest hit they could get. Camels were about the only unfiltered cigarettes easily available. Some gaols will allow you to take things in to prisoners, some won't.

I had other things—my mobile, a laptop and a Smith & Wesson .38 revolver. No Uzi, no shotgun. I hadn't fired the .38 since I'd been relicensed to carry it and I didn't want to start now, but Jobe Tanner had a formidable reputation. Even if Braithwaite was right and Tanner had ways to learn about Twizell's visitors, those networks—of prisoners, ex-prisoners and gaol staff—tend to be slow, and I hoped to be in and out before he got wind of me.

Four hundred kilometres isn't a long round trip, but my Falcon had a lot on the clock already. Besides, there'd been times when I'd set off expecting to be back in two days and had been away for a month. I had the car thoroughly checked over. I had a worn tyre and an air filter replaced and considered whether to charge them to Wakefield. It depended on how things panned out. He was certainly up for the cost of the petrol.

The car behaved itself and the traffic cooperated so that I made good time on the Great Western Highway out of the Sydney basin and over the Blue Mountains. It got colder, but that works for an old engine. I stopped for lunch in Katoomba at the Blue Moon café, that carried memories— some good, some bad—and pushed on, listening to a couple of Lead Belly CDs I'd bought cheap at a garage sale in my street. eBay has cut the legs out from under garage sales and this one had been a flop as they mostly are now, but there was a good selection of CDs and DVDs and I bought some, promising myself I'd find time to listen and watch.

Lead Belly sang: *There's a man goin' round takin' names* and I couldn't help thinking that's what I did a lot of the time. The road had some rough spots and the thumping six-string guitar music seemed appropriate, especially as Huddie Ledbetter had spent a good part of his life in prison.

I rolled into Bathurst in the early afternoon expecting that nothing much would have changed since my last visit maybe ten years before, and I was right. Bathurst was created by the gold rushes of the 1850s. Like Bendigo and Ballarat, it has expanded, but again, like them, with its solid, Victorian centre, it seems to have resisted fundamental change. I booked into the first central motel I spotted and Wakefield's bill went up a serious notch.

Strictly speaking, a private detective arriving in a country town would be wise to check in with the local police. But there are times to do this and times not to. Braithwaite had warned me that the Tanners kept an eye on Twizell and it was more than possible that the Bathurst police did the same. That's not to say that the two interests intersected, but they might. The police and the crims need each other the way fleas need a host and I wasn't keen to advertise my presence any more than necessary.

I made sure the shower, television and radio worked, tested

the bed and checked the mini-bar, a feature of Australian motels unknown in the rest of the world. The trick to countering the depressive sameness of motel rooms—the bland décor, the plastic fittings—is to make it as untidy as possible by scattering your belongings around, especially books, newspapers and magazines. Within a few minutes I had the bed rumpled, shirts hung over the backs of chairs and a table carrying a paper open at the crossword and a bookmarked copy of *Lord Jim*. I was going back to the old guys.

I was stiff from the drive and I wandered around the streets for a while to get the kinks out. It was cold with a sharp breeze and I upped the pace to keep warm. Back in the motel I plugged into their connection to use the laptop to check for emails. Nothing important. I took some of my prescribed pills and poured myself a solid scotch to offset the indignity. That gave me an appetite and I went to a nearby Indian restaurant with Conrad for company.

I had battered cauliflower for an entrée and goat curry for a main. The food was good and the small carafe of house wine washed it down well. Jim was getting himself deeper and deeper into trouble. I'd seen the film many years before; Peter O'Toole was well cast, but the book was a good deal darker than the film.

Wakefield had asked, or rather told, me to contact

him as soon as I reached Bathurst. But I was still irked by the feeling that he had an agenda I wasn't aware of and I was taking petty revenge by delaying the call. I dialled his mobile and got a message. A few minutes later the text came through:

Ask him what he remembers about his paternal grandparents.
Ask him where they were living when he was young.
Ask him about the family Bible.
Tell him there could be a six figure sum for him if things work out well.

Experience has taught me that when people deliver messages with more than one clause, the important subject is in the middle, not at the beginning or the end. Wakefield really wanted to know about the Twizell family Bible: so, I had to admit, did I.

I slept the way you do in motels when you're on your own, especially after a few drinks. You miss the usual house and neighbourhood sounds that reassure you subliminally, and you need at least one piss. I got up at 3.30am and couldn't get back to sleep. Again, as in most Australian motels, the bedside lights weren't well placed for reading. I turned on the television, flicked through the channels and turned it off. I couldn't find Radio National, the only station I ever listened to. I did the crossword and eventually fell asleep just as light was showing through the dusty venetian blinds.

As a person accredited by a legal practitioner I was permitted to visit in the morning; others could only visit in the afternoon. The gaol was three kilometres west of town and I was in the parking area at 10am sharp. The place would have been forbidding enough on a bright sunny day, but the heavily overcast sky and gusting cold wind gave it an extra air of gloom. I'd read up on it a bit. The sandstone gate featured a hand-carved lion with keys in its mouth, supposedly a symbol of the might of the law. They were keen on that sort of thing in Victorian times when the gaol was built. As they will, prisoners found a way to undercut the symbol—legend had it that when the keys fell from the lion's mouth all the prisoners would be freed. The gaol had had a foul reputation as harsh and ill-run until the prisoners rioted in 1970 causing enormous damage. An official inquiry brought reforms and, as far as I knew, it now ran on the standard lines.

I'd been briefly on remand in Long Bay gaol in the past and had served a short sentence in Berrima, and I'd visited clients, friends and enemies inside, so I knew how to behave in a prison. You have to desensitise yourself to sounds, sights and smells. The absence of freedom sits like a cloud of smoke in the air and nothing on the outside resembles the sensation of waiting for the door behind you to be locked before the one in front of you can be opened.

I went through the procedure of divesting myself of keys, mobile and coins. The supervising officer was a woman.

'Can I give him the smokes?'

'The prisoner will receive them later.'

'Can I trust you?'

There's a TAFE course for correctional officers; they probably have a technique for removing the sense of humour.

I was conducted down corridors smelling of institutional cleanser to a windowless room with a lino-tiled floor and walls in the same grey shade. There were three tables and six chairs and heavy staples set in the floor near three of the chairs for the prisoners to be shackled if necessary. There was a clock mounted high above a door opposite the one I had come through. There are lots of clocks in prisons and they don't offer comfort.

The door opened and a guard escorted in a man I had to convince myself was John Dalgarno Twizell. I thought I was accustomed to the impact prison makes on people, but I was shocked at this man's appearance. Four years ago he'd been stocky, running to fat and aggressive-looking, now he seemed very different. His green overalls hung loosely on him because he'd replaced the fat with lean muscle and the fuck-you look of his staring eyes and shaved skull had changed to a calculating smirk. He had shaggy brown hair.

The guard backed away to the door, out of earshot of low voices, close enough to step in if there was trouble. I stuck out my hand.

'Cliff Hardy.'

He ignored the hand and stared past me.

'Mr Braithwaite says hello.'

49

'What do you want?'

I studied him; it was hard to believe he was the same man as in the photograph I'd seen. I had the feeling that the thug was an act and that this composed character was the real man. I was pretty sure Wakefield planned to exploit him in some way and I was prepared to play my own game if it came to that. On the other hand, he didn't look like a victim.

'You must be having a bloody great time in here, Johnnie,' I said.

That reached him. His pale eyes screwed up and his thin lips twisted into a sneer. 'Yeah, I'm doing great.'

'It's funny,' I said. 'I was told you had charm.'

A transformation came over him. He squared his shoulders and expanded his chest; he patted his hair into place, smiled broadly and slapped some colour into his grey cheeks.

'Now, Mr Hardy,' he said in a pleasant, almost tuneful voice, 'it's a great pleasure to meet you. Sorry I can't get you a drink or perform a few other civilities. How's the world treating you today?'

I nodded. 'I get the point.'

'Do you? Charm is bullshit. I could always turn it on and off like a tap. Look where it got me.'

I wasn't going to let him snow me. 'I understood drugs and booze got you here.'

He laughed, still in his positive, engaging pose. 'They helped, they certainly helped, but I'm not blaming them.'

'You're going to do well with this act at the parole hearing. When's that again?'

Some of the brio went out of him. He slumped a bit in the chair but much of the animation stayed in his face. 'Why're you here? Old Courtenay gave up on me a long time ago, I thought.'

'He's the one who said you had charm, but this is about something else.'

He tensed, looked suddenly alarmed. 'I've got you now. You're the private eye who tried to blow Paul Brewer away and would have if the gun had fired. He's in here. He talks about you.'

It had happened a few years ago. Brewer had killed my lover, Lily Truscott, and I'd tried to kill him. It was one of the things that had cost me my licence. I hadn't expected to come up against those memories again. I'd slotted them well away, I thought. It was Twizell's turn to put me off balance.

'That's right,' I said slowly. 'I . . . was off my head at the time. I didn't know Brewer was here and I don't give a shit about him now.'

'You used Braithwaite to get in to see me. The Tanners—'

'Relax, it's nothing to do with the Tanners, at least not directly.'

'That doesn't sound too comforting. What the fuck *is* it about?'

I felt I couldn't just put Wakefield's questions to him without any context and I had the outline down pat now after telling it to Megan and Braithwaite. I gave Twizell an even more edited version, stressing his family connection to an important historical event without being specific. The animation he'd shown stayed with him more or less and he listened intently.

When I'd finished he leaned back and smiled.

'Are you telling me I'm related to some aristocrat and in line to be Lord Twizell of Twizell fucking Hall? Always thought it was a weird name. Wasn't there some guy way back tried to claim a fortune that way?'

A film about the Tichborne claimant had been on television not too long ago. I'd seen it and so, apparently, had he. A young aristocrat on his way to Australia in the nineteenth century had gone missing, believed drowned, and a man had turned up years later claiming to be him. He had supporters, but was eventually exposed as a fraud and went to gaol.

'No,' I said, 'nothing like that, but there's talk of some kind of document, a letter or a journal or some kind of writing, that's historically important. I have a client who wants to find it and if you can put him on the right track there could be money in it for you.'

'Not much use to me now.'

'When you get out. You know and I know that getting back on your feet after a gaol stint is . . .'

'A slippery slope to climb.'

'Nicely put. The ancestor we're talking about is said to

have had a way with words. Maybe you're a chip off the old block.'

'Don't ... what is it? ... *patronise* me,' he said. 'You've given me the first thing to interest me in this fucking hole apart from what the Tanners had in store for me. I was trying to close every fucking thing out. We've still got a while. Tell me more.'

6

I put the first of Wakefield's questions to Twizell. It wasn't a response to his request, but I didn't want to lose control of the agenda.

'Grandpa Bob and Grandma? Jesus, they were ancient, or that's how it felt when I was a kid. They were pretty old. He had some tatts. He'd been a sailor. There was a story that he owned some ships once but not by the time we came along. He was just a retired sailor. Not a bad old bloke. He used to give us money. Grandma? She was quiet; pretty well educated, I think. She read a lot of books. I remember that they were both pissed off at my dad. He was a loser.'

I put the next question.

'They had an old dump of a cottage out of Newcastle near the beach. They reckoned it was historic. Grandma had a vegie garden and Grandpa Bob went fishing all the time. I suppose they had a pension, but they seemed to live on vegetables and fish. We used to stay there when Dad was off somewhere and Mum couldn't handle us, and we got fucking sick of fish, I can tell you.'

'Do you remember the address?'

His eyes went shrewd. 'I might, why?'

'Could be important. What do you know about a family Bible?'

I was watching closely and, although he tried not to react, he could not quite control his eyes. The lazy, out-of-focus stare he'd been affecting dropped away for a split second when he blinked.

'Hey, what're you talking about? I don't know anything about a Bible.'

'Yes, you do,' I said. 'And my client has authorised me to say that a six-figure amount could be due to you if . . . things work out.'

'That's very vague.'

'Do you have anything more solid to think about just now, Johnnie?'

He leaned forward and all the cocky aggression I'd seen in the after-trial newspaper photograph was back in his face and body language. 'You bet I do, arsehole—getting out of this place.'

I shook my head. 'Year away, if you're good.'

'I've *been* good, bloody good, and they've brought my parole hearing forward. It's on next week.'

'Well, good luck.'

'No, these bastards play games with you. There'll be a hearing and you get your hopes up but they'll knock me back for sure. You never get out on a first hearing, the blokes in here tell me. That's unless . . .'

He paused strategically.

'Unless what?'

'Unless someone with clout puts in a good word. Hey, I bet your guy's rich or a museum dude or a professor or something, and you've got old Courtenay onside. They could swing it.'

He was a lot smarter than anyone had thought.

I left the prison with only Twizell's proposal to take back to Wakefield. He wouldn't be pleased. The odd thing was that it didn't feel like failure. Twizell wasn't likeable but neither was Wakefield and I'd be interested to watch the interplay between their devious minds if it went that way. It all might end right there for me, but, again, it might spin out for a time and earn me some money.

While I'd been inside the car park had filled up a bit with a variety of vehicles including vans and utes apparently making deliveries to the prison. I reached my car, felt for my keys and was suddenly aware of three men emerging from the station wagon parked next to the Falcon. They arranged themselves to block me into the space between the vehicles. One, a compact type in early middle age, wore a suit, the others jeans, T-shirts, jackets. One of them was very big, another was rangier.

'A word with you,' the suit said.

Two I could possibly have handled, even in the confined space, but not three. I leaned against my car with my hand not too far from the radio aerial, a possible weapon.

'Okay,' I said.

The suit shook his head. 'Not here. Come with us.'

'I don't think so.'

I reached for the aerial but the lean, wiry one was too quick for me. He chopped down savagely on my arm, numbing it. The one behind me moved up and pulled my other arm halfway up my back. There was no space to kick or head-butt.

'You've done this before,' I said.

'You bet we have,' the suit said. 'And we've done worse. Be smart.'

Being smart meant getting into the back seat of the station wagon between the one who bent my arm and the suit while the other guy drove. I sat, working my arm to restore the circulation, and cursing myself for not being more careful.

'Who do I have the pleasure of meeting?'

'There's no pleasure involved, Hardy, not for you or us. My name's Joseph Tanner. Who my friends are doesn't matter.'

'It matters to me. Someone hits me and someone else bends my arm, I like to know who they are before I get even. I'm funny that way.'

There was an amused snort from the arm bender. I leaned

forward; he reached to pull me back and I slammed my elbow as hard as I could into his ribs. He gave a gasp, coughed and fought for breath.

'I had to make an exception in his case.'

Tanner took a small pistol from his pocket and pressed it against my knee. 'Settle down. You all right, Clem?'

'Let me . . .'

'No. Maybe later. We'll see how it goes.'

The driver said, 'What's going on?'

'Nothing,' Tanner said.

'What's wrong with Clem?'

Clem was gasping as he breathed.

'I think he's got a broken rib,' I said. 'Maybe two if I did it right. I'm not sure.'

'Fuck you,' Clem gasped.

'It's okay,' I said, 'I've had a few. They hurt for a while but they get better.'

'Shut up, Hardy,' Tanner snapped.

I did. Part of my chatter was nerves and it was important to get that under control. We were back close to the town now, moving through suburbs and then into an area of shops and light industry. The van turned and went up a lane. It stopped at the back of what looked like a small warehouse. The lane dead-ended a little further on and there were no obvious signs of activity.

'Out,' Tanner said. 'Any trouble from you, Hardy, and you'll be sorry.'

I nodded in keeping with my stoical decision and took in everything I could see. The thing to do in these situations is to know the ground, spot weapons and, if possible, play some of the people who have you off against each other.

Again, I was in a confined space with three men who had no love for me. One disabled, but one with a gun. No time for heroics. The driver opened a door at the back of the building and Tanner shepherded me in with Clem, wheezing, bringing up the rear.

Boxes stacked high around the walls, windows too dirty to allow in much light, fluorescent tubes glowing. The place had a concrete floor with red paint worn mostly away by feet and time. The man sitting in one of a set of three deckchairs could only have been Tanner's brother—similar hard lines to his body and face, similar suit. A couple of years older, perhaps, and more controlled.

Joseph grunted something unpleasant I didn't catch and slumped into one of the chairs. The older, more composed brother gestured for me to sit. He waved away Clem and the driver.

'Hector Tanner,' brother two said. 'You've met my brother Joseph.'

'I've had that pleasure.'

'He's a smartarse, Hec. I don't reckon you could believe a word he says.'

Hector looked across to where Clem was crouched, holding his side. 'What's wrong with Clem?'

'Hardy cracked one of his ribs.'

'I told you to be courteous.'

'He's a smartarse who thinks he's a tough guy.'

'Not really,' I said. 'It's just that Clem was underexperienced at this sort of work.'

Hector smiled. 'I'm not.'

I shrugged. 'We'll see.'

'Have you any idea why we've brought you here?'

I shook my head. 'You're not doing so well, Hec. I'm not playing that game. You talk to me to start with, not the other way around. If you've got something to say to me, say it.'

'You've been to see Johnnie Twizell.'

'Have I?'

'What about?'

I shook my head.

Joseph shifted in his chair. 'We can make him answer.'

'Doesn't matter,' Hector said, then turned to me: 'I expect you'll be seeing him again.'

'I expect I will.'

'I want you to deliver a message to him.'

'Come on,' I said. 'You know so much you've obviously got connections inside the gaol. You can get a message to him any time you like.'

Hector unbuttoned his jacket and relaxed. Good technique to ease the tension. He was right, he knew what he was doing. Joseph was still tightly strung. 'No,' he said, 'he wouldn't believe a message coming from us through our normal channels.'

'I can understand that. I suppose Jobe Tanner's your father. He threatened to kill Twizell.'

'Well, that's part of it,' Hector said. 'Dad was upset because of what Johnnie did to Kristie, but we don't feel that way.'

'Kristie's a slag,' Joseph said. 'She deserved what she got.'

'Nice,' I said.

Hector shot his brother an angry look. 'I wouldn't put it quite like that but you're right. It's not nice. We're not nice people, can't afford to be.'

'I won't argue with that.'

Joseph growled and tried to swipe me with a backhander. The numbness in my arm had eased off. I caught his wrist, twisted and he had to fall off his chair to prevent his wrist being broken.

'Stop it!' Hector snarled.

The driver had come forward and looked ready to join in but he stopped when Hector spoke.

'Back off, Rog. Let him go, Hardy. There's no need for this. Let's keep it civilised.'

I laughed and released Joseph's wrist. I got to my feet and turned towards Rog. 'I owe you one, mate. Want to have a go?'

'No one's having a go,' Hector said. 'Calm down, all of you. Let's have a drink.'

He had a briefcase by his chair. He opened it and took out a bottle of vodka. Not my favourite but a drink just then seemed like a very good idea.

'Find some glasses, Rog, and, Clem, you'd better go and see a doctor. Get your ribs strapped up.'

'I could do with a drink myself, Hec,' Clem said.

Rog rummaged in a cupboard and came up with some plastic glasses.

'Not too elegant,' Hector said, 'but a drink out of your boot's better than none at all.'

He lined five glasses up on the arm of his chair and poured them half full. 'Just the one for you, Rog, you'll be driving Mr Hardy back to his car.'

Rog and Clem knocked back their drinks and left the building. Hector handed me a glass. 'Cheers.'

The three of us drank. It was good, smooth stuff. Hector poured another three generous measures. 'We're not going to have any more trouble here, are we, Hardy?'

'Depends on what happens when you stop being all hospitable and tell me what message you want me to deliver and why.'

'Fair enough. First, we don't intend to kill Johnnie or hurt him in any way. Second, tell him that we're willing to offer him protection and assistance when he goes for the money.'

I found myself repeating what Twizell had said to me. 'That's very vague.'

'He'll know what it means.'

'I don't suppose you'll tell *me* what it means—just to help me be more convincing.'

'You're an irritating man, Hardy. A little of you goes a very long way.'

'I've been told that.'

Hector nodded. 'I'm sure it's one of your techniques, part of your stock in trade, as it were.'

He was right there. I finished the drink and stood. 'You're out of your mind, Tanner. I'm leaving. If Rog comes anywhere near me I'll put him in hospital.'

His voice had a whip-crack quality. 'You'll do as I say.'

'Involve myself in a criminal conspiracy with a few wannabe gangsters like you? No chance. I've got a job to do and I'll do it. Just that.'

He shook his head mock-sadly and took a mobile phone from his pocket. 'There's 385 grams of high grade cocaine in your motel room. One call and the cops'll be there with the sniffer dogs. I've checked on you, Hardy. You've done time and been suspended and had your fucking licence lifted. You got it back on a technicality. You walk a fine line. I bet there's quite a few cops who'd be happy to see you go down—again.'

He had a point. My reinstatement as a PIA came about as a result of a technicality and there were people who were unhappy about it.

'Supposing I don't go back to the motel?' I said.

Hector sipped his drink. Joseph smirked. 'There's always your car, your house, your office, your daughter's flat, for that matter. We've got a law and order government now, I'm happy to say. Might be a bit hard to convict, you might hang on to your licence if things went your way, but it wouldn't do much for your business.'

'What's to stop me agreeing and then not delivering the message?'

'We'll get a reaction from Johnnie when you do. No question about it.'

Joseph must have thought he'd played second fiddle too long. My guess was that he'd done it from infanthood. He was wearing a nice suit as well, after all, if a bit less classy than Hector's. 'Stuck for words?' he said. 'That makes a welcome change. You've got no real choice, Hardy. And what's your problem? You deliver a message, walk away and never hear from us again, right, Hec?'

Hector didn't like not being the spokesman. Didn't like his brother very much, possibly, but he played along. 'Right.'

I sat down. 'How about another drink while I think about it?'

'Why not?' Hector filled my glass. I held it up and then poured it slowly out onto the dusty cement floor.

'You prick,' Joseph said, half rising from his chair.

'Easy,' Hector said. 'Just as a matter of interest, what were you seeing Johnnie about?'

I stood and moved towards the door. 'It was about money. Maybe a more attractive offer than yours.'

Hector didn't react but my reward was a worried frown on Joseph's face. I opened the door and looked back. Hector waggled his mobile phone at me. He wouldn't unravel under pressure as quickly as his brother, but he was probably the more dangerous of the pair.

I had no idea where I was. I walked down the lane. No sign of Rog, Clem or the station wagon. I went towards the loudest traffic noise and walked until I reached a small shopping centre. I located a taxi rank with one cab waiting. I got in and swore when I was asked where I was going. My mind was on Tanner's threat. Bluff or for real? I told the driver to take me to the gaol car park. My manner discouraged any friendly chat he might have had in mind. We didn't exchange a word the whole way.

7

Motel rooms aren't hard to break into. The room keys aren't complicated and, with a bunch of people who don't know each other circulating about, things don't get noticed. Whoever had been in my room hadn't tried to conceal the fact; quite the opposite. Lying on top of *Lord Jim* was a disc of silver foil about the size of a ten-cent piece. I unwrapped it; maybe the white powder was coke, maybe it wasn't. I didn't care. I flushed it down the toilet. Then I made a thorough search of the room and my belongings in case there was a second stash which would have been a cunning thing to have done—and Hector Tanner was cunning personified. There wasn't. I made a cup of instant coffee and sat down to think.

There was no point in going to the police and accusing the Tanners of deprivation of liberty and making threats. They'd deny it and I had no evidence. I could do as they said, give Twizell the message and get on with the job Wakefield had hired me to do. That went against the grain: I was being threatened and blackmailed. I'd been used to threats ever since I'd got into this business but blackmail was something new. I felt in my guts that if I gave in to it I was finished.

The first thing to do was buy some time. I rang the gaol and arranged to see Twizell again. I assumed the Tanners' contact would let them know that. The next step was to find some way to neutralise the threat. The Tanners were based in Newcastle and I had contacts there—a PIA named McKnight who I'd worked with in the past, and Marisha Henderson, a journalist on the *Newcastle Herald* who'd been a friend and colleague of Lily Truscott. I rang and arranged to meet Pete in his office at Hamilton that evening.

While Pete was wary, knowing that I needed something from him, Marisha sounded genuinely pleased to hear from me.

'Hello, Cliff,' she said. 'Hey, it's been too long. What's up?'

I told her I was going to be in Newcastle that night and wanted to talk to her about Novocastrian matters.

'Like what?'

'Bad guys.'

'Right up my street. Dinner?'

'Has to be later.'

'Come to my place. How long are you in this shithole for?'

'Don't know. I thought you were glad to get the job in Newcastle.'

'I was. Now not so much. Anyway, we can talk about it.

I hope you're still drinking. Not one of these born-again teetotallers, are you?'

I said I wasn't. She gave me the address. A mental picture of her formed as we finished the call—tall, slim and energetic with a slight and attractive overbite. Lily had said she was my type and she was, but at the time Lily was all I needed.

It was 3pm and I had a four-hour plus drive ahead of me. I checked out, paying for two nights, and headed north after topping up the tank and washing down a couple of No-Doz with black coffee. I headed north-east, picking up the Bells Line of Road, keeping a close watch in the rear vision mirror for the first stretch, but there was no tail. I paid a toll for the short run on the M2 and got onto the Newcastle freeway. I played a series of CDs, mostly blues. Hummed along or sang when I knew the words. I was tired from the meeting with Twizell, the confrontation with the Tanners and having to concentrate on the driving, but the caffeine kept me alert.

Pete's office was in a block on the site of a building more or less demolished by the 1989 earthquake. The façade had been preserved. It was well situated but modest, suggesting that Pete was making a living but not getting rich. He was an ex-policeman, invalided out with a pension after being shot. He was ten years younger than me but looked every day of his age. He got slowly and stiffly to his feet as I came into his office.

'How's it going, Pete?' I said.

'Up and down. You?'

'Okay.'

I sat and we exchanged small talk for a minute or two. Pete's hair was thinning as his body thickened. I knew that he was divorced and that his wife had taken the two children interstate. There were signs of work being done in the office but not a lot. The last time we spoke, Pete had told me he missed the bustle of police life but was still heavily dependent on the force for the jobs they threw his way. He'd had some funny stories back then, but he was much less chatty now.

'I've run up against the Tanners,' I said. 'Hector and Joseph.'

'Be thankful it wasn't Jobe.'

'I'll keep that in mind. Joseph's not much, but Hector's got something about him. Would you agree?'

He grunted but didn't say anything. For what seemed like the hundredth time I sketched the job I was on, the message I was supposed to deliver and the threat that came with it.

'Couple of questions,' I said. 'Do they have the resources to plant coke the way they say—the supply, contacts in Sydney, good break-in people?'

Pete nodded. 'They do.'

'I need some leverage against them.'

'Why not just do what they say? No skin off your nose.'

I didn't answer. He looked at me and sighed. 'Of course—you'd reckon they'd own you.'

'Something like that. Hector mentioned my daughter. That made a difference.'

'Hardy the hero.'

'Hardy the pissed-off. You've worked here a long time, Pete. You've got an in with the cops; you know the scene. You know the informers. Shit, operators like the Tanners've got as many enemies as friends, maybe more.'

'That's true and I've been one. But the smart thing to do is stay clear of them. What they've threatened you with is nothing compared to things they've done.'

'Like?'

He shook his head. 'You don't want to know. I can't help you. It's a good thing you didn't mention the Tanners when you rang. I wouldn't have been here.'

'That bad?'

'That bad. In fact I'm worried about you coming here. You asked about contacts—they've got 'em, all over.'

'Jesus, Pete, you used—'

'I used to have more balls.'

I got up. 'I'm sorry.'

I wasn't quite sure what I meant when I said that. I had a mixture of feelings. But Pete took it in the worst way. His sagging face went red and a tic started in his cheek. He knotted his hands together on the top of his desk to stop them from shaking.

'You pity me, right? Fuck you.'

I moved towards the door. I heard him suck in a deep breath.

'Cliff.'

I turned back.

'Don't say you weren't warned.'

'About who in particular?'

His troubled voice sank to a whisper. 'About every one of the fuckers. They're a volatile lot. I doubt that any one of them trusts the other.'

'Not unusual in a crew like that.'

'Yeah, but if anyone tells you Jobe's a spent force, don't believe it.'

'Sounds as if you—'

'Just an observer.'

My nod didn't mean I believed him.

I'd thought my session with Pete would have taken longer. I thought he might have filled me in with some details about the Tanners, might even have taken me to meet a useful person or two. I didn't anticipate that he'd be so reluctant to help. I was there so briefly I could've had dinner with Marisha but she'd have made other arrangements by now so I had time to kill.

I drove into the city centre. Newcastle wore a rundown look and I recalled reading that a plan to spend millions on a revamp had fallen through and that the money men, local authorities and the state government were still trying to thrash out a deal. It looked overdue; road markings were faded, the buildings were rust-stained from leaking guttering and everything seemed to need an injection of money and ideas.

I found a parking spot and had a meal in the first decent-looking eatery I came to. Fish, as recommended by my cardiologist and generally my preference anyway. A half-bottle of white wine to go with the food and wash down the necessary pills. Service was slow, which suited me. I read some Conrad and scribbled some notes. Black coffee to finish.

I bought a bottle of wine at a pub, programmed the GPS and followed the directions to Redhead on the coast a bit north of the city. Marisha's address was a block of flats on the road that ran along the beach. If she was up high enough and in front she'd have a view across the road, the dunes and the beach straight out to the South Pacific Ocean.

It was just after nine o'clock when I buzzed her flat. She released the door after telling me to come up two flights. I went up slowly—you don't want to arrive on a woman's doorstep puffing. She had the door open waiting for me. No ceremony. She stepped forward and wrapped her arms around me. I hugged her and felt a surge of feeling that'd been missing for a long time.

She hung on to my arm and pulled me inside. I hadn't seen her since Lily's wake when she'd been one of the most distressed people there before she became one of the drunkest. She hadn't changed much—still looked as though she could do a triathlon the way she used to. She seemed reluctant to let me go and I wasn't struggling. I waved the bottle of red.

'Good one,' she said. 'Let's crack it and drink a toast to Lily. How are you?'

I knew what she meant. The name had to come up and she'd done it in the best way possible.

'Healed,' I said.

'Jacket off, have a seat, I'll open the plonk.' She looked at the label. 'Shit, that set you back a bit.'

I put my jacket on the couch on top of a pile of newspapers and magazines—the room was pleasantly untidy, a bit like Marisha herself, who wore a wrinkled skirt and a shirt half tucked in, half out.

'My client, you mean.'

She unscrewed the cap on her way to the kitchen. 'Yeah, I heard you were working again. Having fun?'

She came back with two glasses, put them on the coffee table in front of the couch and poured. Then she sat in a chair across from me but not far away. She raised her glass.

'Lily,' she said, 'from two who loved her.'

We drank.

'I asked if you were having fun.'

'It's a good question. I haven't thought about it.'

I was having trouble thinking about anything except her smooth olive skin, dark eyes and the way her overbite gave her a smile all her own. I drank some wine to stop from staring at her.

'Some of it's fun,' I said. 'Some of it's a bit like what you do—talking to people, finding things out.'

She nodded, still smiling. 'But there's a difference. I haven't been shot ten times.'

'Nowhere near ten.'

We drank and didn't talk for a minute. I pointed to the curtains drawn across floor to ceiling windows. The flat was at the front of the building. 'Must be a great view.'

'You don't want to talk about the view, do you, Cliff?'

'No.' I finished the wine, stood and moved towards her. She put her glass down and I took her hands and pulled her up and towards me. She came smoothly and we kissed as if it was something we'd rehearsed. She tasted of wine; she smelled of the sea.

'You've been swimming,' I said.

'Every night.'

We kissed again. We pressed close. I was getting hard.

'Lily said—'

'I know. She told me. She said I was your type.'

'You are.'

'Come on, then.'

We were both eager but not impatient. We took our time and discovered what pleased us both the most. Then it became urgent and we fucked vigorously. After we finished we lay wrapped together in the semi-darkness. She ran a finger down the pale spots that marked where they'd split me open.

'I heard about this but I forgot about it just now. Didn't seem to cause you any trouble.'

75

'It doesn't. Mind you, if we'd done that, say, a day or two before the heart attack, you'd have had to heave me off and give me CPR.'

'I'm good at that. Anyone who does a triathlon should know how to do it. I've done it twice to blokes younger than you who didn't know their hearts were iffy.'

'They say I'm good for quite a while yet if I look after myself. Which I do, more or less.'

'You look pretty good. Not much flab.'

'None at all on you.'

'I'll get the wine.'

We sat in the bed and drank the wine. We filled each other in on what we'd been doing over the past couple of years—solid journalistic work for her and plans for a book on crime in the Hunter Valley, and some interesting cases for me in amongst the routine stuff.

Marisha was still on the right side of fifty; I'd crossed that line. We stayed close, but the days of multiple fucking were past for both of us. We fell asleep before even getting near to talking about why I'd contacted her.

I woke up alone in the bed and had the momentary feeling of not knowing where I was or even who I was. But the sensation passed almost immediately. The bed was warm from Marisha's body and retained her scents of sea, sweat and sex. Light flooded into the room through the open door.

I pulled on my boxers and went into the sitting room where Marisha was standing by the big window with the curtain drawn back. She wore a blue silk dressing gown.

'There's your view,' she said.

It was all I thought it would be—a busy road contrasting with silent dunes, an empty beach and the ocean rolling away forever. I put my arms around her and she rested back against me.

'It's why I bought the place.'

'Wise move.'

'I'll make some coffee, then you can tell me why you're here.'

She was slipping back into professional mode. I told her I needed to get some pills from my bag in the car. I had a quick shower, dressed and got the pills. I arranged them in the palm of my hand and ran the tap for a glass of water. She watched me as I swallowed them.

'Every day?'

'Every bloody day.'

'You didn't bring the bag up,' she said. 'Not planning to stay? Love me and leave me?'

I kissed her. 'Not this time.'

'Meaning there'll be others?'

'I hope so.'

She began to spoon coffee into a plunger pot. 'Me too. So what's on your mind?'

'More who.'

She smiled. 'There's no one else around, if that's what you're thinking.'

'Glad to hear it, but I was thinking of Jobe Tanner.'

She dropped the scoop and coffee spilled over the bench. 'My God! How the hell did you know?'

8

When she'd calmed down, Marisha explained that Jobe Tanner was one of the principal sources she was using for her book on crime in the Hunter Valley.

'This is utterly hush-hush,' she said. 'Until now literally no one knows about it.'

I had to wonder about that after what Pete had said.

'How did you get him to talk?'

'It wasn't easy. Took almost a year of negotiation. But eventually things fell my way. He's getting old and he's found religion. He wants to go out with a clean slate—well, a cleaner one.'

'He's snitching?'

'Not exactly. He's not naming names. Not of live people, that is. Plenty of dead ones. He's pointing me in the right directions, showing me how things were done.'

'*Were* done?'

'Are still being done, but not by him. Now you have to tell me why you scared the shit out of me. What've you heard?'

I tore a paper towel from the roll, put it under the lip of the bench and swept the coffee grounds into it while I thought what to say. I tapped the grounds into the pot. 'I haven't heard a single thing about Jobe doing anything but being the tough, controlling bastard he has the reputation for.'

'What then?'

I explained about being pressured by the Tanners without saying much about what had taken me to Bathurst. I told her I'd seen Pete McKnight.

'Pete keeps himself informed,' I said, 'and when I said I needed a counterweight to Hector and Joseph he just stressed Jobe's name.'

'How do you interpret that?'

'One, that there's friction between father and sons and I'd already got a whiff of that. Two, that he believes Jobe is what he's always been. That suggests your secret is safe.'

'Mmm, maybe. I really need this coffee, then you can tell me what you want me to do.'

She made the coffee, warmed some croissants and we sat at the kitchen table. She was still anxious and I could understand why. If word got out that Jobe was talking there would be some very nervous and nasty people around. I was undecided about what to ask her. The last thing I wanted to do was add to her anxiety.

'I suppose I was going to ask if you knew anyone who knows him and could help get me to see him, but now . . .'

'I'll think about it. How long can you stick around?'

'Not long. I'm supposed to see the guy I went to Bathurst to see pretty soon.'

'You haven't said much about him. Should I know more?'

'Just this—the Tanner brothers are hoping to make some kind of big score with him when he gets out. Do you know of anything that might fit that picture—a drug shipment, a big robbery take unaccounted for, a scam that needs a finishing touch?'

'I'll think about that as well. Are you looking for a connection between the Tanners' interest in the guy in prison and your client's interest in him?'

'I can't see how there could be. Boil it all down and the events are separated by over a century. But I have to consider the possibility.'

We fixed on where and when we'd meet later and left the flat together. Marisha drove off in her Subaru without telling me where she was going or asking me what I was going to do. She kissed me goodbye, but a lot of the heat had gone out of things on her part. It couldn't be helped; she was involved in something delicate and dangerous and I'd blundered into it. She had to decide whether helping me was worth the risk. That meant weighing a lot of work against something very new and maybe ephemeral. The odds were against me.

I located a swimming pool with a gym attached and spent

the morning working out and struggling through twenty laps.

I was walking to my car, thinking about lunch, when my mobile rang. Wakefield. I realised I hadn't contacted him after my meeting with Twizell.

'Hardy.'

'I thought I'd have heard from you before this.'

'I'm sorry, things got complicated.'

'Complicated how? Did you put my questions to him?'

'Yes, and I'm sure he knows something, but he's bargaining with us. He wants you to use your influence to . . . help him at his parole hearing.'

A pause, then an impatient grunt. 'Well, tell him I will.'

'I think he'll want something more concrete.'

'That'll take time.'

'That's what he's got.'

'Are you trying to be funny?'

'No, and my sources were right, the Tanners are keeping a close eye on him and they're putting pressure on me.'

'To do what, kill him?'

I laughed. 'No, it's not clear what they have in mind. I'm in Newcastle trying to find out.'

'You're *where*? You're supposed to be in Bathurst.'

'As I said, it's complicated.'

'Hardy, if you're trying to string this out . . .'

'Listen, Professor, some very nasty people have threatened me and my family. I take exception to that and I'm trying to deal with it, but it's connected somehow to Twizell. I'm dealing with different parts of one thing here, I think.'

Something about my tone of voice must have made an impact. I could almost see him moving the phone away from his ear, backing off. When he spoke again his voice was placatory.

'I'm sorry. I have faith in you. When do you see Twizell again and what exactly does he want?'

I told him and he said he'd try to pull some strings. I said I'd call him after tomorrow's meeting with Twizell and that was it. He'd shown no interest in my statement about a threat. I opened the car door and froze when I saw another little foil package sitting on the seat. I took a tissue from my pocket, used it to pick up the foil, blew my nose on the tissue and went to the nearest rubbish bin to drop it in.

I got in the car and began to worry. No surprise that the Tanners had reach in Newcastle, but how did they know I was there? And if they'd picked me up yesterday, had they tracked me to Marisha's place? If that wasn't enough to worry about, I could always turn my attention to Wakefield. He seemed indifferent to the Tanners. Was that just single-mindedness, or did he know more about the Tanners and the state of things in Newcastle than he was letting on?

I didn't feel like eating but I had to fill in the time somehow and I thought I'd go back to the place where I'd had dinner the night before. I was a few blocks away from it when a police car cruised up and waved me into the kerb. One of the uniforms got out while the other sat with his radio phone at the ready. I wound down the window and put my hands in clear view on the wheel.

'Could I see some ID, please, sir.'

I showed him my driver's and PIA licences.

'I'll have to ask you to accompany us to the station.'

'Why?'

'I'm sure they'll tell you when you get there. Are you going to cooperate?'

'Can I follow you?'

'We'd prefer that you didn't.'

They do that. Sometimes it's because they want to look the car over, sometimes because, in this day and age, a man without a car is just that much more vulnerable. Hard to tell which in this case. He stepped back as I opened the door and rewound the window. You lock this model Falcon with the key. I was about to do that when he stopped me.

'I'll take the keys. Someone'll collect the vehicle.'

They were interested in the car.

Newcastle police station was on Watt Street, not far from the harbour in one direction and the ocean in the other. There were other institutional buildings nearby, like the Anglican cathedral and a hospital. The building had the unimaginative, solid lines common to most police stations. The detectives' room, to which one of the uniforms took me after doing some business at the front desk, was tidy, unlike some, and dominated by clicking computer keys, like most.

The uniform conducted me to a corner of the room where a man sat at a desk with his hands folded, watching our approach.

'Detective Inspector, this is Cliff Hardy.'

'Right. Any trouble?'

'No, strikes me he's done this before.'

'I bet. Okay, thanks, Bill. Have a seat . . . Mr Hardy. I'm Kerry Watson.'

I nodded and sat. He was fortyish, red-haired and freckled, a little overweight in a dark blue shirt that was a bit too tight. He looked tired; his desk was covered with files and sheets of printout and there were post-it notes stuck here and there on the shelves. If I'd had to deal with all that I'd be tired too.

'When did you arrive in Newcastle?'

'Why am I here?'

'Let's get a few things sorted and I'll tell you. You're licensed for a firearm. Where is it?'

'In my car.'

'I'm not sure that's legal.'

'It's unloaded and secure. Your boys'll find it if they're any good.'

'They're good.'

'That's one thing then, what else?'

'What's your business here?'

'You know better than that. My business is my business.'

He shook his head and a few dandruff flakes dropped onto his shoulders. 'Not really. It's customary for people in your . . . line of work to check in with us when you arrive. You didn't.'

'Customary doesn't mean you always have to do it. I wasn't planning to stay long.'

'How long?'

I shrugged. 'Depends.'

He took a notebook from the pocket of his jacket hanging over the back of the chair, turned a few pages. 'You paid a call to Peter Wilson McKnight.'

'That's right. Can we stop this? What's going on?'

'McKnight was found dead in his office this morning. He'd been shot through the head.'

9

Watson watched closely for my reaction and I didn't have to pretend to be shocked. He sighed and flicked through his notebook.

'Your car was spotted in the parking bay of McKnight's building at 6pm.'

'Right, and I left about thirty minutes later.'

'Can you prove it?'

'I went straight to a restaurant in Market Street and would've been there before seven. I've got the bill.'

He nodded. 'For your expenses.'

'Yeah.'

'Must be nice.'

'When was Pete killed?'

'Pete? You were good friends?'

'Not really. He was always Pete, the way Pete Sampras is Pete.'

'Who? Oh yeah, the tennis player. Before Federer. He was killed around 10pm. Where were you then?'

'With a friend.'

'Name?'

'Not unless I have to. You don't really think I killed him, do you?'

'No, but it might be helpful for you to tell us what you wanted to see him about.'

'I don't think so.'

'He's no loss, anyway. Did you know McKnight was a bagman for the Tanners?'

'No.'

'You're surprised?'

'I haven't seen him for quite a few years. People change.'

'For the worse in his case. When his wife left he got on the piss, started gambling, got in deep with the loan sharks. One thing led to another.'

'He didn't look particularly prosperous.'

'No, the Tanners probably bought him by paying off his debts or putting them on hold. They like to control people on the cheap. That's their speciality.'

He wasn't telling me much I didn't know apart from the information about Pete. He put a few more questions to me which I deflected. His heart wasn't in it. When an ex-cop-turned-private-detective forms an alliance, however reluctantly, with criminals, you have a recipe for trouble. Pete's killer would have to be looked for in a dozen different directions and the police didn't have the time or the motivation. When Watson took a phone call, responding in a series of grunts, my interview was over.

'Your car's in the back parking lot. Your keys are at the desk. If any information that might help us comes your way, get in touch.'

I said I would, collected the keys, located the car and drove a few blocks at random to see if I was being followed. Nothing. The contents of the glove box had been left on the seat and I had to assume the police had found the catch that opens the lockable section I'd had Hank install behind the glove box. They'd have learned that the gun hadn't been fired recently.

I followed my original intention and went back to the same city restaurant for lunch. I try not to drink before 6pm, but circumstances dictate behaviour and hearing shocking news seemed worth a drink. I had two glasses of red with my focaccia. I hadn't been close to Pete McKnight but I drank a toast to him. Too young to die. His attitude during our talk made more sense now. Maybe he thought he was doing me a favour warning me away from the Tanners and only my disappointment had led him to name the patriarch. Then again, maybe he'd told the Tanners I was coming to Newcastle.

I strung the food and wine out for as long as possible and then took a walk around the harbour, the beach and the city. I got to the coffee bar at the appointed time to find Marisha there already. I could tell by her body language, stiff and somehow hostile, that things had changed.

Still standing, I said, 'What's wrong?'

'You've blown it,' she said.

'Blown what? How?'

She shook her head dismissively. 'I should have known.'

I sat down finally. 'You're not making sense, Marisha. Known what?'

'Lily told me that the one thing that worried her about you was that you were a magnet for trouble. She said you drew it towards you and she had a suspicion that you liked it that way. In the end you . . .'

I knew what was coming. A lot of people thought Lily had been killed because of me and what I did for a living. It wasn't true and I thought Marisha knew enough to understand that. I'd run into the problem too many times to be angry and now I was just disappointed. That must have showed because she relaxed some of the tightness in her expression and let her shoulders sag.

'I'm sorry, I shouldn't say . . .'

'You shouldn't *think* it. It's not true. But I didn't know she felt like that about me. She never said.'

'She loved you.'

We sat in silence for a while. Then she picked up her computer bag and handbag from the floor and stood.

'You heard about Pete?' I said.

'Yes, and about you being taken in by the cops.'

'Just for a talk.'

'I'm sorry. I can't bring you and Jobe together. Not after today. Goodbye, Cliff.'

She walked out with her long athlete's stride and didn't look back.

Two disappointments for the price of one. A waitress who'd hovered and then withdrawn, probably thinking she was witnessing a lovers' quarrel, approached with a tentative smile. I ordered coffee I didn't really want just to accommodate her.

I toyed with the coffee, thinking how badly things that had seemed so promising had gone. I was no closer to getting something to play off against the Tanner brothers. Pete McKnight had implied a serious rift between them and the father and that seemed likely to widen to a yawning gap if they found out what Jobe was up to. Promising, but I couldn't reveal that without bringing Marisha into the picture. I needed something solid to neutralise the Tanners, get some cooperation from Twizell for Wakefield and bow out of the whole thing.

If contact with me had brought about Pete's death, although I couldn't see how, I was sorry. And I was sorry to lose Marisha's confidence. But sorrow doesn't solve problems. The only thing to do was return to Bathurst. Just possibly, Twizell might give me something to deflect the Tanners.

I did the drive in a sombre mood and I did it reinforced by the blues. I checked back into the same motel. Same room even. I was distributing things about when there was a sharp knock on the door.

I was back in hostile territory so I'd brought the .38 in from the car. I put it within arm's reach behind a curtain and opened the door. A tall woman wearing a leather coat stood there with her fist raised to knock again.

'Cliff Hardy?' she said.

'Yes.'

'I'm Kristie Tanner. I have to talk to you.'

I stepped back and motioned for her to come in. The butt of the pistol was sticking out from under the curtain. She noticed.

'Jesus,' she said, 'you're jumpy.'

'Yeah, thanks to a meeting with your brothers.'

'I know about that. Roger told me.'

I pulled out a chair for her. 'Roger?'

She unbelted and took off her coat. She wore a dark blue dress, short and tight on her generous figure. She was well above average height but her very high heels made her look even taller. Her features were good but they had a slightly heavy, mannish quality. Her hair was brown and short; she wore a lot of makeup, skilfully applied. She moved purposefully, a bit like brother Joseph, as she dropped the coat over the back of the chair and sat.

'Roger Tarrant, he . . . drives for Hector.'

I shoved the pistol into my overnight bag. 'Oh, Rog. Yes, I've met him.'

'He said you broke two of Clem's ribs.'

'Two, was it? I was worried it was only one.' I rubbed the arm where Rog had hit me. 'I owe him something too.'

'I wouldn't,' she said. 'He's a dangerous man. Anyway, he's on your side.'

I sat on the bed. 'I'm feeling pretty dangerous myself just now, but I don't understand. You'd better explain.'

'Did you go to see Johnnie about the cave?'

'What cave? And that's a question, not an explanation.'

She took a deep breath. 'Johnnie's a caver, or he was. He says he found a lot of money, all vacuum-wrapped and sealed. Close to a couple of million, he reckoned. This was in a deep cave. He didn't say where.'

My scepticism must have shown.

'It's true. He says he moved it to another cave while he thought what to do. The trouble was, as he was coming back up the cave roof fell in and he was lucky to get out alive. He broke an arm and a leg and hurt his back. He was in hospital for months. That's where I met him. I was visiting a friend. I knew we were related from his name—second cousins or something. Tanners and Twizells, all part of the same mob.

'And he told you this story?'

She nodded. 'Bit by bit. We started a relationship, hands under the bedcovers, screen around the bed when he got more mobile. Like that. Eventually he told me he needed help to get the money out. He knew about my family and he said he needed people like Hec and Joseph. The money was probably stolen; the cave was on private property. He needed equipment after it collapsed and the cooperation of the owner of the land, who mightn't want to cooperate. You understand?'

'He thought Hec and Joseph'd be good persuaders?'

'Yes.'

'So, what went wrong?'

She sighed. 'Got anything to drink here?'

I opened the mini-bar. She opted for vodka with ice—a true Tanner. I had a light beer.

'My bloody brothers,' she said. 'They're greedy bastards. They decided that if they knew where the cave was they didn't need Johnnie. Joseph would've tortured him but Hec wouldn't go that far, partly out of consideration for me, I think. Hec got hold of some drug that makes you tell the truth. They got Johnnie high on booze and pills and shot him up with this stuff.'

She took a big slug of her drink and closed her eyes for a few seconds. When she spoke again it wasn't much above a whisper, as if the memory had constricted her throat. 'Johnnie went right off his head. That's when he attacked me and nearly killed me. He was delusional, I know that. It really wasn't his fault, not altogether. Anyway, he was yelling and I was screaming and Joseph and Hector were yelling and there was blood everywhere. A neighbour called the police and they took Johnnie away.'

I'd put most of the little bottle of vodka in her glass.

She reached for the bottle, added the rest and knocked it back.

'Johnnie punched me and kicked me and managed to use a knife before Joseph got him off me. They rebuilt my face but I'm not as good-looking as I was. They made me look like a transsexual. A lawyer told me I should sue, but I'd had enough of lawyers and doctors by then. As for the rest of me, want to see the scars?'

'You hushed all this up at the trial? About the drugs? He could've got off on diminished responsibility, or at least a lighter sentence.'

'Yeah, and that would've been the end of the money, wouldn't it? Johnnie was prepared to do the time. He'd been inside before. He could hack it.'

'And your brothers were willing to wait?'

'They had no choice. But Johnnie let them know they were out of the picture and they're not prepared to accept it. That's why they put the pressure on you to deliver a message to Johnnie he might believe. But you haven't done it yet, have you?'

'No. I'm seeing him again tomorrow.'

'Will you deliver the message?'

10

Call me self-interested, but my first thought was that this gave me something to work with against the Tanner brothers. The mention of Megan and the sly placement of the coke had pissed me off and countering the threat had become my first priority. But I was still working for a client and I next had to consider how this affected Wakefield's approach to Twizell. I played for time.

I said, 'I thought cavers always worked in pairs.'

'They do. That's another bit of the . . . hassle. Johnnie said he went down with a young Pommy backpacker he ran into at a pub. The Pom said he'd done a lot of caving at home and was keen to have a go here. Johnnie said this bloke helped him move the money but apparently he was caught when the cave roof fell in. He's still in there, buried. That's another reason they needed Hec and Joseph—to deal with the body.'

'Are they good at that, too?'

Since she'd described the matter of disposing of a body as nothing more than a hassle, I wasn't surprised at her reply. 'I think they've had some experience.'

'It's all very interesting,' I said. 'Not sure I believe it, but you seem to. All I can tell you is that it's the first I've heard of hidden money. My business with Twizell relates to something else entirely.'

'Which you won't tell me about.'

I shrugged. 'No, and no need. Nothing remotely to do with what you've told me, but I'm left with a question.'

She was playing with her empty glass, moving it from hand to hand. 'What question?'

'Suppose I was concerned about hidden money, what was the point of you coming to me?'

'You're supposed to tell Johnnie bygones are bygones and that they'll help him in return for a share of the money.'

'They didn't spell it out quite that clearly, but I suppose that's what they had in mind, once I'd convinced Twizell they were dinkum.'

'I want to ask you to tell him the opposite—that they'd rip him right off.'

'Why?'

'I don't want them to have the money.'

I was getting tired of the question/answer format. 'Because you want it—you and Rog, say?'

'Forget it.' She grabbed her coat and took two steps towards the door before I grabbed her.

'Better let me go,' she said. 'Roger's just outside.'

'Let's have him in.' I grabbed the .38 and threw the door open. He stood there, big and dark, tense, but not alarmed by the gun. 'Come in, Rog. We've got things to talk about.'

He ignored that. 'You all right, Kris?'

She retreated back into the room. 'Yeah, he's an arsehole but he didn't hurt me.'

He nodded and came in, shutting the door behind him. His composure threw me a little. I let the hand holding the gun drop to my side but brought it up as he opened his leather jacket.

'Easy,' he said. 'I'm not armed. Rod Templeton, Central Coast Serious Crimes, undercover.'

'Oh, yeah.'

'It's true,' Kristine Tanner said.

'He's convinced you. Let's see him convince me.'

'I can give you some names and numbers.'

'Okay.'

He rattled off three names. One I knew, Ted Power; he'd worked with Frank Parker, my friend who'd retired as a deputy commissioner of police a few years ago. I knew Power had worked undercover in his time and was very likely to be in a supervisory role in that shadowy world now.

I put the .38 on top of the TV. 'I'll check with Ted later. Might as well hear your story now, for what it's worth.'

'You won't believe him,' Kristine Tanner said.

'I might. We'll see. At least I'm willing to listen. Sit down, Ms Tanner, and Rog . . . or Rod, why don't you bring a chair in from outside.'

He knew I was testing him all the way—provisional about believing him and giving him instructions. He handled it well, shot a quick nod to the woman, opened the door, grabbed a plastic chair and brought it in.

I opened the mini-bar and offered one of the little bottles of gin to Kristine, who glanced at her companion and shook her head. I tossed a can of VB to him and picked up my can.

'Let's hear it,' I said.

It wasn't surprising to learn that the Tanners were a major preoccupation of the Central Coast Serious Crimes unit. The father and sons and several cousins were involved in much of the criminal activity over a wide area stretching up towards the Northern Rivers district, west to Orange and south towards Sydney. They were into drug importation and distribution, armed holdup, protection rackets and a lot more. In fact the criminality had extended back two generations and, while several members of the extended family had served gaol sentences, the Tanners had enjoyed what looked like a charmed life.

'Mainly due to police corruption,' Templeton said. 'But that's changed lately and they're under pressure. And when crims come under pressure things tend to happen. You can't provide something, you can't protect someone, you can't settle a dispute. Cracks appear. You'd be aware of that, Hardy.'

I was, and with every word he spoke I was more convinced he was the genuine article.

Templeton went on, 'Hector and Joseph are in trouble. There's no green light, not even yellow, and funds are drying up. They badly need that buried money.'

'What about Jobe?' I said.

Kristine said, 'That's part of what's happening. Dad's old and he's got religion. He was baptised a Catholic and it's sort of come back to nag at him.'

I finished my beer. 'Bit late from what I'm told and from what I've just heard.'

She looked distressed, almost out of her depth. 'Catholics can be forgiven.'

'Jobe knows the old days are gone,' Templeton said. 'Hector and Joseph, him particularly, either can't see it or don't want to. Jobe's trying to ease out of all the crooked connections—the drugs, the payoffs, the money-laundering scams through the clubs. He's trying to keep himself out of gaol and protect Kristie and save Hector and Joseph from themselves.'

'Big ask,' I said.

Templeton hadn't opened his can. He put it on the floor. 'When I said cracks are appearing, I meant it. It was much too easy for me to get on the strength with them. I had the mocked-up credentials all right, but if they'd really checked properly they'd have backed off.'

'Still might,' I said.

Kristine looked alarmed but Templeton shook his head. 'No, they're feeling the heat. A few of their heavies have sloped off to other parts.'

I rubbed the arm where he'd hit me. 'You're convincing.'

'I had to let them make the play.'

'So what do you want me to do? Always supposing I believe all of this.'

Kristine looked tired and stressed. 'Like I said, don't tell bloody Johnnie that Hector and Joseph are on his side.'

Templeton shook his head. 'This is where Kristie and I think differently.'

'What is it between you two?'

Kristine's attitude to him, in her looks and body language, which had been wholly supportive, was now half accusatory, half submissive.

Templeton clasped and unclasped his big hands. 'Look, Kristie came to us with the story, about Twizell and the money and everything. It made sense.'

'So the money's real?'

'We think it is.'

'You *think*.'

'There's been a rumour around for a while that a big shipment of cash being sent from a finance company to who knows where went missing. The word is that it was an inside job and the security firm hushed everything up and wore it, because they had a huge contract about to come their way and didn't want any black marks on their record.'

'What about the people who took the money?'

Templeton shrugged. 'Don't know.'

They hadn't answered my question about their relationship but it wasn't too hard to work out by this point. The undercover guy and the informant fall in love. It happens.

'So,' I said, looking at Templeton, 'what do *you* want me to do?'

'Go along with what Hector's asking you to do.'

They'd obviously had this out before because Kristine's voice was resigned. 'If Hec and Joseph get their hands on that money they'll bugger up everything Dad's trying to do. They'll finance a bloody crime wave.'

'You know Twizell's got a parole hearing next week?'

Kristine looked alarmed. 'You didn't tell me that.'

'He won't pass it,' Templeton said. 'They never get anything out of the first hearing and we can delay the next one if we have to.'

Well, I knew something he didn't know.

Templeton went on, 'We won't let them do what Kristie says. They've already started to borrow money and make promises to people you don't break promises to. If they think they're close to getting the money, they'll get themselves in deeper. When they don't get it, and everyone knows they haven't got it, they'll be finished.'

'Ms Tanner,' I said, 'have you got a deal with the police about your father?'

'She has,' Templeton said.

I looked at Kristine. She nodded. 'Rod's way's safer for Dad and for me.'

Templeton picked up his beer can and lifted the tab. 'It's safer all round.'

'I don't know about that,' I said. 'From what I've seen of undercover cops they don't always know themselves what side they're on.'

'I know,' Templeton said.

11

Templeton explained that the way the brothers had taken him on as a driver-cum-heavy indicated how much pressure they were under. He said the police had arrested the man they were using and it hadn't taken long for Templeton, hanging around with attitude and a fake criminal record, to be recruited.

'You're playing a dangerous game,' I said, 'you and Ms Tanner.'

'Stop calling me Ms Tanner, for God's sake. Makes me sound like some old maid.'

'We know that,' Templeton said, 'but if things work out right . . .'

I couldn't see it happening but hope has its place. The Twizell case had never seemed completely straightforward and now there were a lot of balls in the air, perhaps too many. But I couldn't back out. The Tanner threat was real enough. Going along with them would put that on hold for now and was worth doing on that account. And I still had work to do to earn my fee from Wakefield. I said I'd think it over and let them know. Templeton helped Kristine into her coat and we all exchanged mobile numbers.

'By the way,' I said, 'do either of you know anything about a private detective named Pete McKnight being killed in Newcastle last night?'

'Heard it on the news,' Templeton said. 'I don't know anything more. I could keep my ears open. Friend of yours?'

'No, a friend of Kristine's brothers, or at least working with them.'

'They don't have any friends,' Kristine said. 'Just each other, and not always that.'

They left. I heard two engines start. At least they weren't travelling around together. From what I'd heard about the Tanners having eyes and ears far and wide, that would've been fatal. Dangerous enough as it was, but perhaps less so if the Tanner influence was waning. Templeton struck me as knowing what he was doing, but love is blind. Was he in love?

I tidied up a bit and was getting ready to go to bed when my mobile rang.

'Mr Hardy, this is Courtenay Braithwaite. Your client, Professor Wakefield, has asked me to make some recommendations to Corrective Services about Twizell.'

'Yes.'

'I'm inclined to do it. I didn't tell you, but I always felt there was something odd about the whole matter.'

'Odd?'

'As if the whole story hadn't been told.'

'Is it ever?'

'Sometimes. Anyway, you can tell Twizell I'll do what I can.'

'What does that mean,' Twizell said, 'he'll do what he can?'

'I don't know—talk to the right people, email them . . . Are you behaving yourself these days?'

'I'm a fucking choirboy.' He laughed. 'Hey, you know what I mean.'

It was the first sign of humour I'd seen from him. The little hint of good news seemed to have improved his mood out of all proportion. It's like that in prison, no matter how long or short the sentence—you inflate the smallest flicker of hope, particularly if it carries the promise of getting out.

The guard by the door wasn't paying us much attention, but I lowered my voice and leaned forward. 'I've got another message—from the Tanner brothers.'

He'd been affecting a lazy, relaxed demeanour but that galvanised him. He straightened up and drew in a deep breath.

'Those cunts. What're you doing talking to them?'

'I didn't want to. They grabbed me in the car park here.'

He sneered. 'Grabbed you? Thought you were supposed to be tough.'

107

'Three men, confined space. Bad odds, and then they applied some pressure I'm not in a position to resist. Not just yet. D'you want to hear what they had to say?'

The good humour had vanished. 'Yeah.'

I'd made my decision: I was going with the scenario Templeton had sketched. 'I don't understand it,' I said, 'but they say they want to let bygones be bygones and that they'll protect you when you go for the money.'

His eyes got a faraway look as if he was envisaging scenes and conversations in the distant or not so distant future. He glanced at the guard, who gave him a hostile stare in return.

'That's something to chew on,' he said with the faraway look back in place.

I waved my hand in front of him to get his attention. 'Back to the business in hand, my client's matter. He's come some of the way towards you.'

'Yeah, I suppose.'

Clearly the Tanners' message had claimed top place on his agenda. If he had hopes of the Tanners they'd be balanced by misgivings, but a couple of million dollars would draw the focus of most people.

The guard looked up at the clock. Not long to go.

'The Tanners'd rob their grandmothers,' he said. 'But I wouldn't mind talking to them. You get a day release organised and we could do that.'

'It'd be closely supervised.'

'There's ways. I have to thank you, Hardy, although I'm

sure you're a bastard at heart. You've given me something to think about apart from counting the fucking days and weeks and months.'

'So glad,' I said. 'Now how about my business?'

'Yeah, there was a family Bible and all sorts of letters and shit. Talk to Kristie, she knows more about it than me.'

I'd learned something of this from Kristine but it wasn't the time to say so. 'How come?'

'We're related, third cousins twice removed or some such shit. My grandma and hers were sisters, I think, or cousins. Anyway, she's the one who knows about the family history.'

He realised what he'd said and covered his face with his hands. 'Jesus, I've blown it. Your bloke won't give a fuck about me.'

I was thinking fast. The business with the Tanners and the buried money was no affair of mine, but I had a score to settle with them over the threat. And I felt some guilt about Pete McKnight's death and regret about Marisha, and it was all connected. I wouldn't be able to let it all drop.

'No,' I said. 'A deal's a deal. I'll try to make sure he sticks to it.'

When I got back to the motel I looked through the documents Wakefield had given me and confirmed the Tanner–Twizell family connection Kristine and Johnnie Twizell had referred to: William Twizell's de facto wife and the mother of his son. It was a long time back, but in those days people tended to remain in the one locality and marriages between cousins and less closely related people were common down through the generations.

It was going to take time to ease the restrictions on Twizell, if it could be done at all, and I had nothing better to do than to pursue the written account that was supposed to put flesh on the bones of the second survivor of the *Dunbar* story. I had Kristine's mobile number and I rang it.

'Kristine, this is Hardy.'

'Kristie, for God's sake.'

'Kristie, I need a number for Hector to tell him I've delivered the message.'

'Why would I help you do that?'

'Come on, it's probably the best way.'

'You fucking men. You always know what's best, don't you?'

'Not always, no.'

'Mr Cool.'

She gave me the number. 'Is that it?'

'No, I need to talk to you about another matter entirely. Can we meet somewhere?'

'Oh, yeah, sure, I've got nothing better to do than run around after you and get Hector and Joseph all suspicious.'

'Sorry, but it's important. What do you do for a living?'

'Nothing. I've got a disability pension. Johnnie left me with some impaired movement. What d'you want to see me about? Planning to double cross . . . somebody?'

'Nothing like that. It's about history. A shipwreck.'

There was an electronic silence, then she said, 'Are you serious?'

'I am, yes.'

'All right, I'll meet you. Not at the motel, though. Some-where on the road back to Newcastle or the boys'll start wondering why I'm here.'

'What have you told them so far?'

'Mind your own business. What are you, a detective?'

She named a pub I'd seen on the way out of Bathurst and agreed to meet me in an hour.

I rang Hector.

'Hector Tanner?'

'Could be. Who's this?'

'Hardy. I delivered the message to Johnnie.'

'What did he say?'

'He said it gave him something to chew on.'

Hector chuckled. 'It so happens I know you're not lying. We've . . . I've had a message from him myself that says he has hopes of getting some outside time soon. That your doing, Hardy?'

I imitated his tone. 'Could be.'

'Are you taking the piss?'

'No, if I ever get the chance I'll make you sorry you

threatened me the way, you did. But for now, with a job on hand, can I assume your threat to me is dropped?'

'Call it on hold. Just keep the fuck out of it.'

He cut the call. There were a lot of things Hector didn't know. He didn't know I knew about the buried money. He didn't know one of his minions was a cop. He didn't know that I'd have to keep monitoring Twizell at least for a while, and he didn't know I was about to meet up with his sister, who wished him no good. That was too much ignorance for someone in his position and could make him dangerous. Trouble was, there were things I didn't know, like who killed Pete McKnight and why, and whether Marisha's dealings with Jobe Tanner were as secure as she thought.

Kristie came towards where I was sitting in the pub. She had her leather coat belted tight and moved confidently in her high heels. I wondered what work she'd done before Twizell put her on the disabled list. I got up politely and she almost sneered.

'A gentleman, are you?'

'Sometimes. D'you want a drink?'

'Why not? Vodka and ice, slice of lemon.'

I realised I hadn't eaten anything since breakfast. I bought two packets of chips, her drink and a red wine for me.

'It's a picnic, eh?' she said.

'Knock off the tough act, Kristie. We're in a complicated situation. We've got two dead people . . .'

She sipped her drink. 'Like who?'

'The backpacker Twizell left in the cave. It must have crossed your mind at some time that he was expendable, given the amount of money supposed to be involved and Twizell's record. And there's my private detective contact in Newcastle. That could be connected to this business.'

'I suppose.'

'So let's be serious. I've just heard Hector warn me off. If he found out your friend Rod's in touch with me . . .'

'Okay, okay. You're right. I'm scared and the tough act is . . . camouflage.'

'What did you do before—'

'Before Johnnie sliced me up? I was a marine biologist—well, a marine biologist's assistant. Doing a part-time degree. No more diving for me. Among other things, Johnnie punctured a lung and ruptured an eardrum. Shit, I've lost the thread. Why're we here?'

After all that had happened I'd lost the slick version of Wakefield's story I'd trotted out before. Now I put it together again as best I could without giving away too much.

'My client's a historian. He wants to find out some things about the wreck. There's been some talk of a written account and mention of a family Bible. Twizell knew what I was talking about when I mentioned that.'

'Yeah, he would. He told you we were related?'

I nodded. We'd been sharing the chips and drinking. It was almost convivial.

'Twizells and Tanners hooked up a few times over the years. We're probably a bit inbred. Might account for how crazy some of us are.'

'The Bible.'

'Grandma Tanner's cousin had one. She was a Twizell. By the time I saw it, it wasn't really a Bible—all the guts had fallen out of it.'

I sighed and finished off my wine. 'Bugger.'

She smiled and her heavy features changed and I could see how attractive she might have been before the surgery. 'No, no. It was just sort of a shell of the thing, like a big folder. There were lots of papers inside—letters and . . . documents. I had a quick sneaky look once and there was something about a shipwreck. I was interested because I'd dived on wrecks.'

'What was in the papers? Letters, photos?'

'Could be.'

'Come on, this is important. It's why I'm here.'

'You're here, big deal. What's important to you might not be important to me.'

'What *is* important to you?'

I realised that was a hard question for anyone to answer at any time. She stared at her clasped hands and said nothing.

'Kristine?'

'It was years ago but I was interested in it as a kid and they took notice of that. Most kids, especially the boys, couldn't have cared less about old women and their stuff. All they cared about was their cooking and what money they could screw out of them. So, in a roundabout way, it came to me when the old girls all dropped off. I had a quick look at the stuff then but . . .' She touched her face. 'It was before all this happened. I just forget what was in them.'

12

I had a surge of hope that I might be able to complete this part of the business at least satisfactorily. 'And where's this stuff now?'

She smiled again. 'Well, I'll have to think about that. Is it worth any money?'

'It could be. That's between whoever actually owns it and my client. That is, if it's really what he's looking for.'

'How much?'

'No idea.'

'You've been on the job a while and I imagine you don't come that cheap. Must be money in it, but I'm more interested in trying to keep you on our side. Rog . . . Rod says there's talk that Johnnie could be getting out soon.'

'Jesus,' I said, 'd'you realise how dangerous it is for you two to be chatting back and forth on your mobiles? I suppose that's what you've been doing.'

'We take precautions.'

'You'd better. So, how do you want to play it from here, Kristie?'

She got up. 'I'll let you know. Thanks for the drink and the chips.'

She walked out, cinching in her belt and ignoring the appreciative looks she got from some of the drinkers. As things stood, she had the upper hand. Searching for a card to play, I remembered that Twizell had mentioned his grandparents' historic cottage. But 'historic' could have just been a figure of speech. In any case, where was it and which grandmother? I was thinking about this when my mobile rang. I looked at the incoming call number—Marisha.

'Cliff, I'm sorry I blew up at you. I need your help. Something terrible's happened.'

'Tell me.'

'Jobe's been shot. I was with him and I got him to the hospital but he's in a bad way. Now everyone knows I've been talking to him and there's a man here . . . Joseph, Jobe's son, who's waiting for me. I'm scared to move away from where I am. From the look he gave me and the way he talked to the doctor, I . . . I think *he* might have shot his father or had something to do with it.'

'I'll come,' I said, 'but I'm some hours away. What about the police?'

'Two detectives came and wanted me to go with them but I wouldn't. I faked a faint and a panic attack and I'm in a room under observation. I'm not completely faking. I'm bloody scared.'

'Did you know the cops?'

'No, not really. I mean, I know who they are. I know they *are* police, but after what Jobe's told me about how things work I couldn't trust them.'

I knew where the hospital was from my visit the day before and told Marisha I'd be there as quickly as I could. I got on the road and was grateful the late afternoon weather was fine and the traffic was light. Having driven it just the day before, I was confident of the route and able to keep the speed up to the limit and beyond.

I tried to sort out in my mind what this meant in the current state of things. Marisha's cover was blown and she was definitely in danger. Whatever information Jobe Tanner had given her, Joseph and Hector—perhaps Joseph in particular, as the more volatile of the two—would want to suppress. If Marisha's suspicion was right, perhaps he had tried to suppress it the hard way. Turning up in support of Marisha would arouse the Tanners, but there was nothing to be done about that.

As I drove I used the hands-free phone system Hank had installed to call Rod Templeton.

'This is Hardy. Can you talk?'

'Briefly. What?'

'Jobe's been shot. Maybe by Joseph. Any ideas on that?'

'Fuck. It's possible. There's been a falling out between

Hec and Joseph. It's to do with your mate McKnight. Joseph found out about . . . I have to go.'

I was on the freeway driving fast. *I'm too old for this*, I thought. Then I remembered how Marisha had looked when she'd wrapped her legs around me and, in a quick mental segue, how bored I'd been in my enforced retirement. I kept the pressure on the accelerator.

The reception area of the hospital was a madhouse. Television and print journalists jostled with police trying to get information from the medicos. I didn't see Joseph but I did see DI Kerry Watson. He approached me with a look that fell short of friendly.

'What the hell are you doing here?'

'Marisha Henderson's a friend of mine.'

'That'd be right. At the moment she's obstructing police.'

'She's probably in shock.'

'Not too shocked to bring you running. She's not taking calls, even from her colleagues.' He pointed to the milling reporters. 'You must be special. What's she told you about Tanner being shot?'

'Just that he was. She also says she can't trust the police.'

He shook his head. He looked more tired than he had before and much less assertive. 'I can't tell you how sick I am of shonky journalists, and lawyers and chancers like

McKnight and busybodies like you getting in the way of me doing my fucking job.'

It was the kind of complaint I'd heard before and always from honest police. Watson looked too worn down to be on the take.

'Does Marisha know you?'

'She does.' He held up his phone. 'But she doesn't . . .'

'She'll talk to me. Can you organise for us to get away from here to somewhere safe and with no . . . prejudice?'

'Meaning?'

'No arrest. No taking her in to help with enquiries. None of that.'

'You're not asking much.'

'She's a strong character. She'll stall; she'll bring in her editor and her doctor.'

'Okay, okay, but I get to hear what she has to say.'

'I hope so.'

'Jesus, Hardy, you're an operator.'

Marisha responded to my call and Watson and I went through to where she was being treated in a casualty ward. We negotiated with a doctor and nurses and were shown through a series of passages to a back door. We used my car to get to Watson's flat in Hamilton, not far from where Pete McKnight had had his office.

Watson lived alone in a nondescript building. The flat was

untidy in a comfortable way that had a calming effect on Marisha.

Every time I'd seen her, apart from when she was drunk at Lily's wake, Marisha had been in complete control, formidably so, which probably helped to account for her still being single. She'd been a reporter for close on thirty years and had seen some rough things but now she was shaken. Watson, who'd barely spoken other than to guide me to the address and escort us to the flat, produced a bottle of Johnnie Walker. Marisha's hand shook as she drank. Neither Watson nor I needed to ask what the brown marks on her cream linen jacket and blue skirt were.

'He was sitting right across from me,' she said, more to herself than to us.

Watson spoke gently. 'This is where? We'll have to . . .'

Marisha shook her head. 'I can't tell you.'

'Ms Henderson, I—'

'Easy,' I said. 'Let her tell us what she can.'

'I wasn't meaning to say anything.'

'Look, Marisha, your life's in danger. You and I both know why.'

'I don't,' Watson said.

It took time and Marisha was very economical with information. She'd been with Tanner in what she called a safe house. She said she'd been blindfolded by Tanner when he took her there so it wasn't that she wouldn't reveal the address, she couldn't.

Watson's patience was eroding. 'You must have seen where it was when you left.'

'I was in a panic. I just didn't notice.'

Watson wasn't convinced and neither was I, but he would know a journalist would be selective with the truth. He nodded for her to go on.

'He wouldn't let me call an ambulance. I suppose he had a tame doctor to go to. He didn't say. He drove away with blood everywhere until he almost passed out. I just managed to ease him onto the passenger side and I drove to the hospital.'

Watson grunted. 'That was sensible.'

'He won't be happy.'

'Why d'you care whether a crooked old fart like Jobe Tanner is happy?'

Marisha flared, recovering a good measure of her composure. I tried to soothe them both by getting Marisha to describe anything she could about the person who'd fired the shot.

'Two shots,' she said. 'I think the second one was for me but Jobe pulled me down despite . . .'

The shakes returned. After more whisky she repeated what she'd said to me. She had a feeling Joseph Tanner was responsible for the shooting.

'A feeling?' Watson said. 'That's not worth a—'

'Based on what?' I said.

'On how he looked at me at the hospital and what Jobe's told me.'

'Jesus,' Watson said. 'If you've got inside information on a war between Jobe and his sons, I want to know about it.'

'One son, probably,' I said.

Watson was swilling the last of his drink and almost spilled it. 'What the fuck do *you* know about it?'

It was a tricky moment. The more I learned and heard about the Tanners, the more I seemed to get drawn into their machinations and steered further away from what I'd been hired to do. I had dangerous information myself—knowledge of the cop inside the Tanner network and the sister's role in the scheme of things—and I didn't feel able to reveal any of that. On the other hand, I wanted to get as clear of it all as I could and coming semi-clean to Watson was a way to do that.

Watson wasn't dumb. 'I can see your beat-up brain working, Hardy. You're wondering how many lies to tell.'

'No,' I said, 'I'm wondering how to protect Marisha and myself and my client's interest first and then how to help you.'

'Thanks a lot.'

'I'd like you to nail whoever killed Pete McKnight.'

'Oh, that'd be a sort of bonus, would it? You're a scavenger, Hardy.'

'I'm tired,' Marisha said.

I looked at Watson.

'There's a hotel we use. You'd both be safe there.'

I put my hand gently on Marisha's slumped shoulder. 'And you'd be able to keep an eye on us.'

'Give me something, for Christ's sake,' Watson said.

I wanted to talk to him about stolen millions and a missing backpacker, to get some corroboration of Templeton's and Kristine's story, but it wasn't the right time.

13

The hotel was of a higher standard than I expected. There was room to move around, good lighting and fittings, and even white terry-towelling bathrobes. Marisha took a very long shower and wrapped herself in a robe as she watched me making coffee.

She was rapidly regaining her confidence. 'Put yours on and we could be like Bob and Blanche.'

'No thanks.'

'You ever think of getting married again, Cliff?'

'Don't see the need. Look at Julia and what's-his-name.'

'Tim. You're right, I never felt the need, ever. Why did you say Joseph might be at war with Jobe but not Hector? What dealings have you had with them?'

'Is this research or . . . ?'

'Oh, shit. I'm sorry. It must sound like that. No, I just want to know to help me work out what to do next.'

What to do next, I thought. Good question. I was sick of holding everything in and I told her pretty well the whole story, stressing that she'd have to get my okay to publish some of the stuff I'd spoken about relating to Wakefield and the supposed *Dunbar* documents.

Colonial history didn't interest her; she homed in on the present. When I finished she said, 'I'd like to talk to Kristie.'

More single-mindedness. 'So you're going on with the Newcastle underbelly stuff?'

'Hell, yes. I need a book to my name. I want to get back to Sydney. I thought I'd had enough of it and coming up here was the right move, but I miss it.'

I could understand that. Couldn't live anywhere else myself, and the prospect of her being back there was attractive. At my age you need all the friends you can get. I decided I'd help her as much as I could, hope the Tanners would resolve their differences one way or another and leave the way clear for me to persuade Kristie to help in Wakefield's quest. It was all a bit speculative but the best I could do.

We ordered a room service meal. Marisha spent a good hour fielding phone calls. She told her editor she'd be filing tomorrow. She fended off other journalists and reassured a few people she was all right. I phoned Templeton. Again, he said he could talk for a short time.

He said, 'I'm about to drive Hector to Newcastle to see his father.'

I said, 'There's a whisper that Joseph fired the shots.'

'He wouldn't. He hires people for that kind of work, mostly. Unless it's very personal. He hired the hit on McKnight.'

'Why?'

'I'm putting this together from bits I've overheard and things Clem's told me when he's pissed. Joseph thought McKnight was edgy. He got someone to pressure him and he learned that McKnight was all set to talk to some journalist Jobe was talking to. Joseph's got too much to hide to let that happen.'

That made it likely Joseph was behind the attack on his father and Marisha. I asked Templeton if he had enough to get Joseph arrested.

'Almost. Things are happening; gotta go.'

Marisha and I went to bed, sleeping comfortably together like a married couple without the need for sex. But it was a different story in the morning.

After a leisurely breakfast we left the hotel soon after ten o'clock and I was surprised that there was no sign of a police presence.

'Some protection,' I said.

Marisha didn't answer. She was staring at a poster outside a newsagency: GANGLAND BOSS KILLED—SON ARRESTED. The story, with photographs, occupied the whole of the front page: Jobe Tanner had died of his wounds in hospital overnight. Joseph Tanner had been arrested on a charge of conspiracy to murder. Hector Tanner was being sought by police.

part two

part two

14

Marisha worked her phone, contacting everyone she knew who might know what had happened and what the official line was. She learned that everything had changed in a few hours overnight. Jobe had identified the man who'd shot him. The police picked him up. Charged with wounding at that time, he had rolled over and named Joseph as the one who'd commissioned the hit. He'd be pissed off and worried later when the charge was upgraded to murder.

From Templeton I heard that there had been a violent confrontation between Joseph and Hector involving threats and weapons. Hector took himself off before Joseph was arrested and Templeton claimed not to know where he'd gone. I didn't know whether to believe him or not. The Tanner crime network fell apart in a matter of days without the lynchpins.

Marisha filed several stories drawing on some of the information she'd had from Jobe. They were picked up by other media and her profile rose sharply. With the threat from the Tanners reduced, she went back to her flat and started serious work on her book. I hung around for the next day with her and we got on well, but her focus was on the book and the rewards it might bring her. I'd developed very strong feelings for her and, in the game of who-can-help-who we seemed to have fallen into, I had one card to play—Kristie.

'I really want to talk to her,' Marisha said.

We were eating breakfast on her balcony on a mild morning with the sun filtering through light clouds and the waves enough to tempt some surfers—black dots out beyond the breakers.

'So do I,' I said. 'But I don't know where she is.'

'You've got her number.'

'Yeah. She's in the book. I tried the landline and went to the address. Nothing. Same on her mobile and the number for her undercover mate.'

'Whose name is?'

I shook my head.

'You're a detective, aren't you?'

'Yes, and do you know what we do a lot of the time? We stir a bit and wait for things to happen.'

'Great.'

It was shaping up as that kind of relationship: good but combative. I'd told her something about the Wakefield matter and my hope that Kristie could be useful. She was only mildly interested. I'd also sketched in a bit about Johnnie Twizell and the buried money. That interested her more as a sidebar to the Tanner story.

'When's his hearing?' she asked.

'Yesterday. I'm waiting for a result.'

'And then what?'

'If he gets out I'll see if he can help with the Wakefield thing. He might even know where Kristie is. They were together for a while.'

'What about the buried money?'

'I don't give a shit about it.'

'I do.'

I reached over and stroked her arm. 'So we'd better stay in touch.'

I drove back to Sydney, checked on things at home and in the office, visited Megan and phoned Wakefield to bring him up to speed.

He struggled to keep the excitement out of his voice. 'Are you saying this woman knows about a set of family papers?'

'That's what she said. I think I believe her.'

'But you don't know where she is now.'

'That's right.'

'My God, Hardy, you haven't exactly carried all before you.'

'There were distractions.'

'Yes, well, I registered the name Tanner and the connection with Twizell. Were you involved in all that gangland business?'

'Peripherally. Did you make representations to the parole hearing?'

'Yes.'

'We should hear results from that soon. Johnnie Twizell knows something about the family history but not as much as Kristine.'

Disappointment replaced excitement. 'So what do you propose to do now?'

'You want me to stay with it? Costs are mounting. You've just about run through your retainer.'

'Of course I do, and that's what you have a reputation for, isn't it—seeing things through?'

'I like to think so.'

'I'll make a deposit into your account. Email me the number. Please try to find that woman.'

'If I do and she has what you're after, she'll want a share if there's money involved.'

'I'll be delighted to discuss it with her.'

More or less out of curiosity I rang Ted Power, the old cop whose name Templeton had given me as a reference. You don't discuss such matters over the phone and Power, a resident of Ultimo, agreed to meet me at my office after he finished work that evening.

I remembered him as superficially calm but underneath highly strung from his own years of undercover work. He'd been shot at least once and bashed a few times and bore the scars like badges. His face was lumpy, ugly. He accepted a large scotch in a plastic glass gratefully.

'Tough day, Ted?'

'Cheers. Tough enough.' He glanced around the room. 'You've picked up a bit since your St Peter's Lane days.'

'So's the rent. I'm glad to have a drink with you, Ted, but I won't piss around—an undercover guy I met up in Newcastle gave me your name as a reference. It was enough to make me trust him, sort of.'

He raised his glass. 'Thank you.'

'I'm going to need to talk to him again so I thought I'd better follow up and get your assessment.'

'You have this place swept?'

'Regularly. Hank Bachelor did it yesterday.'

'I know Bachelor, he's good.' Out of long habit his voice dropped several notches. 'Okay, name?'

'Rod Templeton.'

Power eased his back in the hard chair and took a swig of his drink. 'Roderick Fitzjames Templeton, BA, bronze medal Olympian.'

I raised my eyebrows. Didn't say anything.

'Judo,' Power said.

I rubbed my arm. 'It still hurts where he chopped me.'

'Thought you said you were onside.'

'As far as it went. What else can you tell me?'

'Very tough, very bright.'

'Incorruptible?'

'Who is?'

'Come on, Ted.'

'It's hard to draw the line in that game. Undercover police sometimes have to do criminal things in the course of their duties.'

'I know that, but there are rules about how far they can go and what restitution has to be made, right?'

'Right.'

He drank, I drank. He stared out the window, then he cleared his throat. 'All I'll say is that he pushes the envelope, pretty much the same way you do in your business, Cliff.'

'So you'd advise me to be careful in my dealings with him.'

He nodded.

'There're no bugs here, Ted.'

He finished his drink and got up. 'He's done some very good work and I don't think he feels fully appreciated. Enough said.'

I saw him to the lift and went back into the office and topped up my drink. Pill time. I kept a corresponding supply at the office to those at home, some in the fridge. I squeezed them out of the foils into my palm and took them with a mouthful of scotch. Supplies were low. A chemist in Glebe had half a dozen of my prescriptions on file. Once, feeling resentful, I told him I'd thought of chucking all the stuff away and letting nature take its course.

'You can't do that,' he said, 'I've got children to support.'

I smiled at the memory.

I did my usual Sydney things—paid bills, went to the gym, filled prescriptions, checked that Wakefield had deposited money. He had. Towards the end of my second day back I got a phone call. I didn't recognise the number.

'Hardy.'

'Hey, Cliff, this is Jack Twizell.'

'Jack?'

'Yeah, a new me. You did it, man. I'm out tomorrow and I'll be heading back to Newcastle.'

'Congratulations.'

'You bet. I want to buy you a drink to thank you.'

'No need.'

'And to talk about your proposition.'

'I thought you said Kristie was the one to see about that.'

'Two heads are better than one. Did you see her?'

'Yes.'

'Didn't get far, eh?'

He was riding high, cocky, about to be released and no doubt feeling that the threat from the Tanners was past. Couldn't blame him. I knew I'd have to deal with him but I wanted it to be on my terms as much as possible.

'Only so far,' I said.

'Look, I'm guessing, after all that shit with Jobe and

Joseph, that she's not walking around in the sunshine, am I right?'

I had to niggle him. I had very ambiguous feelings about Johnnie/Jack. I didn't like him much, didn't trust him at all, but I needed him. He was a key player in the game. I wanted him confident and willing to help but not too confident, not feeling a sense of absolute independence. It's not hard to touch a nerve with someone in his position.

'Yeah,' I said, 'on the loose, like Hector.'

It didn't work. He chuckled. 'Don't worry, Hector's in South America by now, or some such fuckin' place. Kristie's a home girl. I can find her. Why don't you come up to Newcastle? Meet me tomorrow and we can talk things over.'

I'd printed out my bank statement with Wakefield's substantial deposit ensuring my survival for another stretch of time. Money confers an obligation; not as big as love or friendship, but an obligation nevertheless. I said I'd see him. Jack had made his plans; he had a place to stay lined up. He gave me the address as if he was installed already and prepared to be hospitable.

15

I drove to Newcastle, booked into a motel and phoned Kerry Watson.

'You again,' he said.

'I've got some business to do with John Twizell. You knew he was out?'

'You bet I knew. He has to check in with us twice a week and report to his parole officer in Newcastle. I doubt he'll have time for anything else. What sort of business?'

'It's nothing to do with the Tanners. It's family history.'

'The family history's bad—his old man was a crook and Johnnie was lucky he didn't kill that girl. He was a small-time crim himself. Don't tell me Bathurst rehabilitated him.'

'I don't know and I don't care. What I'm interested in goes way back. I just thought I should let you know I was around, the way I'm supposed to do.'

'Don't make me laugh, Hardy. You want something. Spit it out, I'm busy.'

My guess was he was always busy—one of those people—but if he had been busy he might know what I wanted to know.

'Any news of Hector?'

'Thought you said you weren't interested in the Tanners.'

'I'm thinking about Marisha Henderson. You probably know by now she's working on a book and I don't imagine Hector wants it to see the light of day.'

'Hector's got bigger problems.'

'Why? I hear he had a big blue with Joseph. Probably very pissed off at having his father shot.'

He sighed. 'Hardy, you know more than you should and you're more fucking inquisitive than's good for you. I'm certainly not going to discuss operational police matters with you. But I'll tell you this—we don't know where Hector Tanner is and if you happen to stumble across him in your fucking around you'd better let us know at once.'

'I won't be looking and I would. I've got a couple of other questions, not strictly related to what we've just been talking about.'

'Have you now? You've got a bloody nerve. Do you know how much work I've got piled up here?'

I didn't say anything, didn't have to. A conscientious policeman like Watson can't suppress his curiosity.

'Go on, then. Make it quick.'

'What can you tell me about a cover-up of a couple of million dollars of stolen money?'

'Nothing. It's just a rumour.'

'How about a British backpacker missing in the Newcastle area?'

'I'm not in Missing Persons.'

'Could you ask around?'

'What's in it for me?'

'I don't know.'

'Why doesn't that surprise me? I don't suppose you've got a name or a date.'

'No.'

'I don't know why I don't arrest you on suspicion of every fucking thing I can think of. Stay out of trouble.'

How many times had I heard that, and from people who thought better of me than Watson.

I met Twizell at a café attached to a squash club in Mayfield. He was wearing the appropriate clothes and glowed with cheerfulness and the virtue gained from hard exercise. He'd had his hair cut stylishly and looked years younger than he had in gaol.

'Haven't played for yonks,' he said, 'but I jogged and did fifty push-ups a day in the slam and I've kept my fitness, more or less.'

I was tempted to suggest he might care to go caving but

I resisted. That was something he didn't know I knew about and I was happy to leave it that way.

'Good for you,' I said. 'Joined here, have you?'

'Thinking about it. Not sure I'm staying in these parts.'

That spoke volumes. He had plans.

'I'm having a decaf cap, what about you?'

'Long black.'

'Toxic.'

He got up and went to the counter to order. He swaggered, only word for it. He chatted to the barista and allowed her to see his sinewy arms and the biceps that stretched the short sleeves of his shirt. He came back with the coffee, wooden stirrers and a handful of sugar and artificial sweetener sachets. He poured two of the artificial sweeteners into his mug and stirred vigorously.

'Now, to business,' he said. 'You want to see Granny's cottage, right?'

'Don't play games with me, Johnnie—'

'Jack.'

'Don't play games. There's something I'm looking for. If you can help me find it, good. If not, just get on with your life and good luck to you.'

The affable manner vanished. 'Listen, I've spent hard time with other people calling all the shots. Well, that's over now and I'm taking charge of things, starting with my name and my health and my bloody future. I've got a clean slate. I don't owe anybody anything.'

His eyes were blazing and his knuckles were white as he gripped his mug. He was irrational, overreacting to a couple of mild remarks. A violent mood swing. It was a new factor to take into account and not a welcome one. I drank my coffee and didn't speak, allowing time for the storm to pass. He fiddled with the torn sachets as he struggled to get himself under control.

'Okay, okay,' he said. 'Sorry, I'm still getting used to this.' He spread his arms and almost knocked over a child who was passing. He spun around and steadied the child, who yelled. A woman bustled up and knocked Twizell's hand away.

'Don't you dare touch her.'

'I was just . . . fuck you!'

The woman stalked away, pulling the still upset child behind her. Twizell slumped in his chair.

'Take it easy,' I said. 'I know it's tough inside but outside's no picnic either. There's a hundred and one things to piss you off every day if you let them. Let's focus on something you can do. Is there any point in going to your grandparents' house?'

He sucked in a deep breath. He had gone pale and it took a little time for colour to return to his face. When he spoke his voice was thin and lacking his previous confident tone. 'I dunno. It was a tumbledown ruin last time I saw it. But I know there were lots of hiding places in it. Grandma used to hide things from Grandpa.'

'What sort of things?'

'Books and that. He used to get cranky about her reading all the time when he wanted her to be working in the vegie patch or bottling fruit and looking after him. He tore up some of her books once and she used to hide them from him.'

'What else?'

'Oh, papers and bills and stuff. He used to throw bills away but Grandma'd keep them and save up to pay them. He was an irresponsible old bugger.'

'I thought you reacted when I mentioned a family Bible.'

'Did I?'

'Yes.'

'Coulda been something like that. I didn't take much notice. Me and Rob used to dig the books out of the hiding places just to watch Grandpa do his block.'

'You sound like a prize pair.'

'We were just kids.'

'Where was this?'

'Out near Dudley. Want to take a look?'

Twizell was driving a Nissan Patrol 4WD, the sort of vehicle you'd need, say, for going off-road and getting near enough to go climbing down into caves. I followed him south for about fifteen kilometres until he parked in a dead-end street of well-established houses several hundred metres back up a hill from the coast. He joined me and pointed to a break in the ti-tree scrub at the end of the street.

'On foot from here,' he said. 'Down a pretty rough track.

They don't let people build down near the dunes any more but there were shacks and cottages there earlier on.'

I was wearing jeans and sneakers with a reasonable tread; Twizell's footwear was something similar and we coped with the steep descent. The track was fairly overgrown but rocks had been embedded in it at strategic places and the trees growing close to it gave me something to steady myself with on the sharpest inclines.

He was right about his fitness. He handled the slope and the impediments better than me. Lizards scampered in the undergrowth and birds chirped in the trees. Traffic noise died away to be replaced by the sound of waves on the beach. The ground became more sandy and we reached a level stretch about twenty metres back from the dunes. The scrub was thick and laced with lantana.

I sucked in a deep breath and looked up as a helicopter buzzed overhead.

'Looking for dope,' Twizell said. 'Spoilsports. Through here. Should've brought a machete.'

He pushed through the ti-tree and waist-high flowering bushes that had almost completely obliterated a track.

'Used to be a way into here from the other direction and you could get a truck down but a landslide wiped it out. There's the house.'

A mudbrick, timber and galvanised iron structure with a collapsed roof and gaps in the sides looked as if it was being held up by the vines that had invaded it. The native vegetation had crept up all around it but there were patches that showed where a bricked path had been and the broken-down wooden fence carried the faint suggestion of a vegetable garden. A mudbrick chimney, wrapped around by wisteria, looked the most solid part of the building.

'Bloody great place for kids,' Twizell said. 'Lots of people used to come here; uncles and aunties and cousins and some we called uncle and aunty but weren't really, you know.'

I nodded. The way it used to be. Now kids called their parents' friends by their first names. Much better.

'Hiding places,' I said.

'Go easy. This is memory lane for me, mate.'

'When you were Johnnie.'

He laughed. 'Yeah, they called me Johnnie B Bad. There used to be a shed and a fibro sleep-out, that was a couple of places, and there were floorboards that came up and some gaps where the gal iron had been tacked on. I'll need some kind of tool to clear a way through all this shit.'

We fossicked around and found a broken garden fork and a length of rusty pipe that had been part of a gate. Twizell pointed the way and we slashed through the grass and bushes to a derelict shed mostly eaten away by white ants. Twizell shook his head.

'That's fucked.'

We worked through to the house but the floorboards had been taken up and the joists and bearers were spongy from the termites. Twizell's neat squash gear was a mess now with smears of dirt, rips from brambles and discolourations from the smashed bushes. My jeans and shirt were in the same condition and our sneakers were muddy from the soggy patches where water had collected.

'Last hope's the sleep-out,' Twizell said. 'Over here.'

We skirted an impenetrable lantana patch and hacked our way through snarly bushes until we felt under our feet some concrete slabs covered with moss. A fibro building stood in the middle of a sandy space with sprouting razor grass.

'Us kids used to sleep out here and get up to mischief.'

'I can imagine.'

'Nothin' much—just smokes and beer and dope—sheilas later on.'

Perhaps because the area was drier, with no trees close by, the sleep-out hadn't been as devastated by white ants. At first glance it looked almost as if it could be made liveable, but on closer inspection the window frames had rotted, the guttering sagged and sections of the iron roof were missing. The remnants of a tarpaulin fluttered.

'Fuck, I remember now. They had a storm and lost some roof. Never got around to fixing it.'

Twizell suddenly seemed depressed by the sight and I wondered what memories he was processing. He threw away the garden fork, went around to the back of the building and crouched by a fibro hutch.

'Dog kennel's still here. She stuck her books inside a sort of cavity. I remember once when we pulled some out she really whacked into us. Grandpa didn't get to see those ones. If she had anything serious to hide this'd be where, I reckon.'

'So why did we piss around with the other places?'

He grinned and wiped a hand across his grimy face where a few scratches had bled. 'Why should I make things easy for a bastard like you?'

I tossed away the bit of pipe. 'Get on with it.'

'Take it easy.'

I was getting sick of him. 'Ever hear of Ross River fever, Jack?'

'Sure. Why?'

'There was a champion golfer got it around here. Blew up over 120 kilos on steroids and cortisone trying to get rid of it.'

That touched his vanity. He was proud of his physique. 'And what happened?'

'He got better but it buggered him for a long time.'

But in the end he was irrepressible. 'Good for him. Getting back to the old girl, she reckoned the dog'd keep Grandpa from poking around and she was right. Claudius, she called him; bitzer with some bull terrier in him. Mean fucker, he was.'

'Twizell.'

'Okay, okay.' He flexed the muscles in his arm. 'You scared of spiders, Hardy?'

'Yes.'

'Me too. Here goes.' He thrust his arm into the kennel

and scrabbled around. He grunted and withdrew his arm. He had a mass of mouldy, cobwebbed paper in his grasp.

'Let's see now.' He peeled back a few layers and let out a screeching laugh that sent birds flying out of the trees. He held out a pulpy handful to me.

'Knitting books. The old bugger hated to see her knitting as much as he hated to see her reading and she could do both at the same bloody time.'

16

Hard to say who looked the bigger mess by the time we'd struggled back up the track to the cars. Twizell was bleeding from scratches to his face and legs; my shirt was a wet rag and my hands were muddy from where I'd had to clutch at the ground to stop myself from falling when the helicopter made a low pass overhead.

'I need a drink,' Twizell said. 'You?'

I nodded. We drove to the Dudley pub—old style with a wide veranda supported by spindly poles. Twizell dropped into a chair outside the bar. 'Schooner of Old, thanks.'

I had the same and we didn't bother with salutations. We both lowered the levels quickly.

'Do your parole conditions say anything about drinking?'

He grinned. 'You ever know anyone bother about that one, either side of the desk?'

'No.'

'Right. But I'd better get back and clean myself up. I have to report to the cops.'

'I'll come with you.'

'Why? Are we pals now?'

'No. You said you could help me find Kristie.'

He finished his drink and obviously wanted another but he looked at his watch. 'I did say that, didn't I?'

'You did.'

'This is important to you, eh?'

'It's why I'm here.'

The shrewd look I'd seen from him before came back into his blood-streaked face. 'Is it really? You've seen her a few times, right?'

I still had half a glass left and I sipped it to buy time and think. How much of what I knew about his pre-gaol behaviour should I reveal?

'Twice, I think.'

'What did she tell you about me?'

'Not much. You're not her favourite person.'

'She'll get over that. How about Joseph and Hector?'

I shrugged. 'Nothing. Just told me to deliver the message.'

'Why would a bloke like you dance to their bloody tune?'

'Threats.'

'Figures. Family man, are you?'

'Sort of.'

'You know I'm at the Mayfield Apartments. You'll find it

in the book. I forget the number. We should stay in touch. I reckon you could be useful to me.'

I shook my head. 'I see it the other way around. You help me find Kristie and then we see if that does you any good.'

'I need protection.'

'Who from?'

'Hector fucking Tanner.'

'You said he was in South America.'

He got up. 'I hear a whisper that he's not. I've got your card. We'll stay in touch, Hardy.'

He practically ran to his car. I let him go.

I rang Marisha.

'You're back, good.'

'Is that glad you're back or you want something?'

'Both. Where are you?'

I told her and she told me the easiest way to get to her place from there. It wasn't far. I wondered about turning up in my dishevelled state but I needn't have worried. She had my sweaty shirt off almost as soon as I walked in and the dirty pants and muddy sneakers soon after. We made a mess of her neatly made bed, which brought it into line with the rest of the room. The bedroom doubled as a study and Marisha was a very untidy worker. The desk was awash with papers and file cards and sheets of printout and photocopies. The paper flowed onto the bookshelves and the floor.

She saw me looking at the chaos and laughed. 'I know where absolutely everything is.'

We were lying close together in the bed. I'd felt something rustling behind my head and I reached under the pillow and pulled out a sheet of paper.

'I knew that was there,' she said. 'I was reading it in bed last night before I fell asleep thinking of you.'

I laughed and did my Bogart. 'You're good. You're very good.'

She jumped out of the bed. 'I'm having a shower and you better have one as well. I'll wash that shirt and stick it in the dryer.'

'Do the socks and the jeans while you're at it.'

A while later we were sitting on her balcony with coffee and fruit salad watching a storm sweep in from the east. The sky and the sea were purple and, as the light dropped, the sand took on a hard, metallic glow. The trees bent to the wind and the rain moved in, turning the road black and the gutters into rushing streams. I couldn't help thinking of the old house in the bush. It must have endured hundreds of such assaults and it was a wonder it had lasted as long as it had.

'So,' Marisha said. 'You turn up here filthy dirty but horny as hell. What have you been doing?'

I told her.

'So the next step is to find Kristie. I want in on that.'

'Johnnie, or should I say Jack, Twizell thinks the next step is to get protection from Hector Tanner. How do you feel about that? Hector can't be happy about you.'

'You're here to protect me, aren't you? Why are you smiling?'

'It's just that I've got a job I'm being paid to do here and now I've got two people asking for my protection.'

'I'll pay you. My agent's negotiated a very good advance for this book. I was just doing it on spec before. I can take some unpaid leave now and knock it off.'

'I don't want you to pay me. How did the agent manage that?'

'I wrote a detailed synopsis and she pitched it really well. She's good.'

'Must be. Did you put anything in about the buried money?'

'Yes, why?'

'Did you mention Twizell?'

'Not by name.'

'What does that mean?'

'I referred to a prisoner about to be released. Hey, why the grilling?'

'The people who stole that money don't know where it is. All this time they'll have been hoping they'd hear something that'd help them find it.'

'They're not likely to hear about a synopsis given to a publisher.'

'Who knows? Your agent might have gossiped; the

publisher probably got its legal team to work. They might have had an outside reader look at it.'

'God, I thought the money was just a footnote to the story, but if those people, whoever they are, come after Hector and Twizell it becomes much more important. By the way, I did some checking and an English backpacker named Roy Flanagan did go missing from around Newcastle at that time.'

The storm hit and drove us inside. Marisha's reaction was squarely in line with her character. Her whole focus was on her book and she'd view events from that vantage point. If Jack Twizell or Hector Tanner were tortured to reveal what they knew, it'd just be useful collateral damage to her. Maybe I should've viewed it in the same way myself, but I couldn't. I had to warn Twizell at least; Hector I cared less about.

Marisha was keen to get back to work. As soon as the worst of the storm had passed I left, wearing my clean clothes still warm from the dryer. She promised to be extra careful in all her movements and to contact me the second she thought she might be in danger.

'You scrub up pretty well,' she said as she kissed me goodbye. 'Go out and find Kristie for yourself and for me.'

The mobile phone Megan and Hank had given me for a birthday present had an internet function I hadn't yet used. I sat in my car and fumbled my way to the White Pages website and got an address and a number for the Mayfield Apartments, which I rang.

'Concierge.'

'Mr Twizell, please. Flat ten.'

'Apartment. Just a minute, sir.'

Sir waited impatiently. When the concierge came back on the line she sounded apologetic. 'I'm sorry, sir. The number doesn't answer. I know Mr Twizell is in because he had a visitor a short time ago.'

'Male or female?' I gave it a conspiratorial tone to which she didn't respond. 'Male.'

'What floor's Mr Twizell's on?'

'He's on the top floor. Is there anything wrong?'

'No,' I said, thinking, *yes!*

Back to Mayfield under a leaden sky. I used the GPS to guide me and found the Mayfield Apartments to be a three-level modern block packed onto a tight bleak cul-de-sac. There were spaces for cars but I wouldn't have wanted to manoeuvre the Falcon into any one of them. The apartments had to be one-bedroom jobs with everything miniaturised that could be. The only thing generous about the set-up was the size of the rubber-tree plants in the tiny garden.

The concierge sat at a small desk in a small tiled lobby. She was thirtyish with a neat, efficient-looking appearance. She glanced up from the computer keyboard she'd been tapping.

'Yes?'

'I rang a little while back for Mr Twizell. Would you try him again, please?'

She frowned, worried, and hit a button on her phone. I could hear the ringing.

'No answer,' she said.

'Did he leave a mobile number with you?'

'I wasn't here when he arrived.'

'Please look. It's important.'

She tapped some keys, found a number and rang it. 'No answer again,' she said. 'What's the problem?'

I headed towards the lift.

'You can't just go up. I'm supposed to notify the residents.'

'You tried,' I said.

I rode the lift to the top floor and got out into a narrow carpeted area. Three apartments up here, with number ten at the front. The lift door closed noisily behind me and the door to apartment ten opened. Hector Tanner stepped out. He was immaculate in a suit and tie as before but this time he was carrying a pistol fitted with a silencer. He pointed the gun at my chest.

'Saw you from the window, Hardy. A pleasure to meet you again.' He gestured with the pistol. 'Step inside.'

17

I walked down a short passage to a living room with windows that looked out to the street. Twizell was sitting in the middle of the room on a chair, with his arms drawn back; both his feet were pinioned to the chair legs by plastic restraints. He was wearing an old dressing gown and looked very vulnerable and afraid. He evidently hadn't had time for a shower since getting back because his scratches were still untreated. He had a black eye and his mouth was puffy with a split upper lip.

Hector pointed to a chair drawn up to the table. 'Sit over there, Hardy, and sit very still. Johnnie and I have been having a little talk.'

I wasn't too worried about Hector's gun. I had my .38 stuck in the waistband of my pants in the small of my back under my shirt-tail. I thought I could distract Hector long enough to get it out and make matters even. 'He goes by Jack now,' I said.

'So he tells me, but I think I'll stick with Johnnie. That's how I knew him when he came to us with a very interesting proposition. That's before he nearly killed my sister.'

'Yeah,' I said, 'after you'd filled him full of some kind of truth drug.'

'True, but he was on something already and the combination did the damage, so it was partly his fault.'

That was interesting. Hector looked to be one of those people who didn't take the blame for anything. A weakness.

I relaxed in the chair and scratched my chin. Best to keep moving in small ways as a preliminary to a big move.

'Why'd you go into hiding, Hec? I wouldn't have thought the cops would have much on a cautious man like you.'

'I didn't go into hiding. I just happen to have a few places to stay that nobody knows about.'

'So you'll show up at your father's funeral tomorrow?'

'I'll have to think about that.'

'But you'll be there in spirit. I wonder if they'll let Joseph out to attend?'

'Shut up. I'm grateful to you for getting Johnnie out early. Now you can help me persuade him to tell me where the money is.'

'Don't do it, Jack,' I said. 'The Tanner mob is finished. They're in debt all over the place and with Jobe and Joseph out of action Hector's fucked. He needs the money worse than you do.'

'He doesn't have a choice,' Hector said. 'I've sent Clem for some bolt-cutters. Persuaders, you might call them. You remember Clem, Hardy. He'll be happy to see you.'

That changed things. I could imagine Clem's enjoyment at the situation. It was time.

'Better tell him then, Jack,' I said.

Twizell's head had been slumped on his chest. He jerked up and shouted, 'Whose side are you on, you—'

Hector focused on him for long enough. I was out of the chair and had my gun free in one movement. Hector swung back towards me but too late. I smashed down on his gun hand with mine; his fingers opened and he dropped the gun. I put the .38 to his temple.

'You wouldn't,' he said.

'You're right.' I moved my hand away, changed my grip and brought the gun butt sharply back against the side of his head. On the button, as the boxers say. His eyes rolled up and he fell hard.

'Jesus, Hardy, thanks.'

I had my Swiss army knife sawing at the plastic restraints before the words were out of his mouth.

'Get dressed quickly and collect up anything you need. We have to get out of here. The guy he mentioned, Clem, is bad news and he has a big-time grudge against me.'

Twizell looked as though he'd like to kick Hector but his bare feet wouldn't do much damage. 'Can't you handle him?'

'Get moving! He's a big bastard. If he came at me with a set of bolt-cutters I might have to shoot him and I don't want to do that on your account.'

Twizell got the point. The last thing a recently released parolee needed was to be involved in a shooting. He bolted into the bedroom and I heard him opening and closing drawers and cupboards. He came out dressed in his suit and carrying a bulging overnight bag.

Hector hadn't moved. I checked his pulse; it was strong and his breathing was regular. I picked up his gun, a Beretta automatic, and stuffed it inside my shirt.

'Let's go! Leave the door open.'

We went down in the lift past the startled concierge. Big Clem was coming up the path carrying a Mitre 10 shopping bag. It seemed like a silly thing to do but I pulled out both pistols and pointed them at him. 'Go up and see your boss. He needs help.'

He gaped, recovered fast and reached into the bag but we were past him by then and running for my car. I had a quick look back as I started the motor. He stood in the middle of the path holding a pair of large bolt-cutters with blue blades and red handles.

Twizell saw him, too. 'Jesus Christ, he'd only have to have taken those things out of the bag and I'd . . .'

We got moving. 'Don't think about it. Do you have anywhere else to go for a while?'

'No. What about my car?'

'If they know what it is, Clem's likely to go to work on it with the bolt-cutters.'

'They don't know.'

'Okay. You can come to my motel and fix yourself up a bit. Then we can go back and get your car. Hector'll have another shot at you.'

'I owe you, Hardy.'

'Blood oath you do, and you can pay me back by finding Kristie.'

I figured protecting Twizell was a justifiable expense, so I booked him into the room next to mine in the motel. He took some time to get himself cleaned up and composed. When he knocked on my door he looked presentable. He'd showered, washed and combed his hair, and the scratches on his face had stopped bleeding. I could smell whisky on his breath. I had the feeling that Jack Twizell was looking to hitch a ride with me for as far as he could. Maybe even as far as the money.

I drove back to Mayfield for his car. Twizell was quiet.

'What's the matter, Jack?'

'Just thinking.'

'About the buried money?'

'Kristie told you, did she?'

'Yeah, you've got a problem there you might not know about.'

'I've got enough to be going on with, but you'd better tell me.'

Without naming her, I told him about Marisha's book and the possibility that information about his hiding of the money was more widespread than he realised. Templeton was in the know as well, but I didn't mention him. No telling who he might or might not have told.

'So?' Twizell said.

'Could be pretty hard people, the ones who stole the money in the first place. They wouldn't have been happy when they found it wasn't where they left it.'

'Tough.'

'Probably kept their ears open for information.'

'I've thought about it.'

'Have you thought about why it was hidden at all?'

'Of course. The serial numbers were on record.'

'But you were willing to go for it straight away. How come? I'm asking just out of professional interest; I couldn't care less whether you get the money or not. Finance companies are just corporate thieves as far as I'm concerned.'

He laughed. 'Got a mortgage, have you? Well, that's one of the reasons I went to the Tanners. They've got connections to launder the dough—sell it at a discount maybe. I'd still have come out with a lot if they hadn't got greedy.'

'What's your move now?'

I caught his sidelong glance. 'Look, Cliff, I said I owe you and I do, but that doesn't mean I totally believe what you say about the money and finance companies, or that I totally trust you.'

I shrugged. 'Believe what you like. All I've got is a mild professional interest in that stuff.'

He didn't reply. We were in Mayfield close to the apartment building. I circled the block a couple of times.

Twizell was alert, checking everything. 'I'll answer one of your questions. It's the time-lapse factor. The security company had the numbers but they'd replaced the money with cash of their own. They didn't give a shit about the numbers. The guys that lifted it must've just waited a while to see how things broke. Didn't look as if it'd been there very long. The money'd still have to be managed, but no one's looking out for it.'

For the second time I realised he was smarter than people gave him credit for.

'Except the ones who stole it and, as I say, word might be getting around.'

'Negotiable,' he said. 'Looks all clear here. I'm going for the car.'

I gunned the motor and shot away.

'Hey! My car!'

'Didn't you say you had to check in with the police?'

'Yes. Next stop.'

'No car, no check-in until you take me to Kristie.'

18

It felt good to be taking some decisive action instead of just reacting to things as they came up. Tight-lipped, I drove a couple of kilometres making turns at random. When I stopped I had no idea where we were. I turned to Twizell.

'Time to stop pissing around, Jack. You put me in touch with Kristie or I drop you here and check you out of the motel. You can swing in the breeze with Hector and Clem and the guys who stole the money after you.'

He checked his watch. 'I'm supposed to see my parole officer in half an hour and check in with the police straight after.'

'You'll make it if we have an agreement, otherwise I'll keep you here and you'll be fucked. Want to add the cops to the list?'

'Okay, okay. As soon as you get me back to my car and I get through the appointments I'll try to take you to her.'

PETER CORRIS

'No way. You're without wheels until the moment I see her.'

'Jesus, Hardy. I said I'd *try.*'

'Try hard,' I said. 'Try very hard.'

I drove back into the city and waited in the soulless building that housed people in what Wakefield had called the custodial industry, while Twizell saw the parole officer. He was in and out very quickly.

'Did he ask about your scratches?' I said.

'She. No, she hardly gave me the time of day. I don't think she liked me.'

We walked two blocks to the police station and I sat on a bus stop seat outside while he went in. I reflected that I'd broken my undertaking to Kerry Watson to tell him if I ran into Hector Tanner, but the circumstances were against it. Tanner said he had places to go that nobody except him knew so there wasn't much point in telling Watson about the encounter now. Next time, maybe.

It was late in the afternoon when Twizell came out of the police station.

'How did it go?'

'Bastards.'

That's all he said. We walked back to the car. I sat with my hands on the steering wheel.

'Well,' I said. 'It's time to find Kristie.'

'You've phoned her?'

'Of course—landline and mobile. No answer. I went to her address. A neighbour said she hadn't been seen since the balloon went up. Is there a friend she'd go to?'

'She had a girlfriend named Michelle who lived in Broadmeadow.'

For the next couple of hours we drove around, visiting people Twizell named and trying various places like a gym, a dance studio and a florist where Twizell said Kristie had worked part-time. We came up empty.

'I guess my information's out of date,' Twizell said.

'Try to think outside the box,' I said. 'Think of somewhere she might go with a lover she wanted to impress or help.'

'Has she got a lover? You didn't tell me that.'

'Think.'

'I could do with a drink.'

'Later.'

We were sitting in my car, parked outside the florist shop in Charlestown. Twizell's fingers drifted up to his face where his scratches had started to scab. He took them away quickly. 'What sort of a bloke?'

'Tough, tougher than you.'

'Tougher than you, Hardy?'

'Yet to be seen. Younger.'

'I get it. I've had a thought. There was this place out in the Humpback Range country. Kristie and that girlfriend in Broadmeadow and someone else used to rent it and share.

171

Hot chicks. You know, go different weekends. You swim and go bushwalking and fish and screw, but there was also this fucking rock face. Must've been, I dunno, fifty metres high maybe. Anyway, Kristie challenged me to climb it. She said she did that with all her boyfriends.'

'You've just remembered this place?'

'Man, I've tried to forget it. I've been in some scary places caving but this . . . I still don't like to think about it.'

'Did you climb it, Jack?'

'I did and I was shit scared every inch of the way. It looked sheer from the bottom and there were really only toe and finger holds in most places and if you fell you hit sandstone hard.'

'Why did you do it?'

He looked at me. 'Why d'you think? She was . . . You've seen her, haven't you . . .?'

'You wrecked her face. They rebuilt it but she's not beautiful.'

He went quiet and thoughtful. I doubted he was remorseful more than just a little. Knowing Jack, he was calculating. 'From what you say about this bloke, I reckon Kristie would be sure to test him. Anyway, it's a nice place to stay, especially if you're keeping your head down.'

'Phone?'

'No.'

'How far away is it?'

'Too far for now and I'd never find it in the dark.'

We went back to the motel, both a bit worn down by the day. I called Marisha's landline, got her voice mail and called the mobile.

'It's Cliff. Where are you?'

'Out and about.'

'I've had a run-in with Hector. He's looking nasty.'

'What d'you mean?'

I didn't want to mention the bolt-cutters. 'Just be careful.'

'Almost exactly what that copper, Kerry Watson, told me.'

'What did he want?'

'Hard to say. Just checking on my story and warning me about Hector. Have you told him about seeing Hector?'

'I'm supposed to have, but, no, I haven't.'

She laughed. 'Always keep the cops guessing. Watson said he'd have his boys keeping an eye on me. I don't like that much.'

'I do.'

'What're you doing?'

'Moving forward.'

She laughed again.

'You bastard. I'll expect more.'

There was a hamburger joint near the motel and we settled for that. Neither of us felt social. We took the food into our own rooms. I watched the news on television and read for a while. About 10pm I knocked on Twizell's door. He was in pyjamas, watching television.

'Let's make an early start,' I said. 'Eight?'

He groaned. I saw several beer cans and miniature spirits bottles on the table. 'Nine.'

'Eight-thirty then. Goodnight.'

I went back into my room and listened. If I'd been in his shoes and was planning to sneak away, I'd have made it look as though I was ready for bed and it wouldn't have hurt to have pretended to be drunk, but I doubted Twizell was playing games. He had nowhere to go and he was getting a free ride from me. I could still hear the TV half an hour later. Then I heard it go off and silence descended apart from the buzzing and humming—traffic and electronics—that seem to be with us no matter where we are.

I slept poorly and woke early. I killed time by Googling the Humpback Range so as to know a bit about where I was heading. There wasn't much information and it didn't surprise me that there were vineyards in the area. It's hard to go anywhere these days without vineyards.

The day had dawned fine. The breakfast I'd ordered for 7.29 came on time. The coffee was hot and the toast wasn't soggy. No sound from next door, which surprised me. I'd picked Twizell as a morning TV viewer.

At 8.20 I knocked on his door and got no answer. I swore and tried the handle. The door was open. The room was a mess. There was no sign of Twizell or his bag. No toiletries. I swore again and left the room. I stood there fuming for a few minutes, then a Nissan Patrol pulled in from the road and up to the slot for Twizell's room. He jumped out and greeted me cheerfully.

'Can't go where we're going in that rattletrap Falcon of yours, Cliff. I hopped over to Mayfield by cab and picked up my car. Then I went for a swim.'

He showed no signs of the night's drinking.

'Why did you take your stuff if you knew you were coming back here?'

He grinned. 'Just wanted to give you a fright.'

'Were you followed?'

That took the wind out of his sails a bit. 'What?'

'I told you Hector wouldn't just give in.'

'Yeah, funny thing is, I thought I was being watched the other day. I suppose that was Hector or one of his blokes. No, I kept an eye out this morning and I don't think I was followed. Tell you what, you can pay for the gas. Ready to go?'

I wasn't and I said so. He took out a tissue and rubbed at a spot on the gleaming duco. I was annoyed at his game-playing and I don't like petrol being called gas, but I couldn't help smiling. One to you, Jack.

We got going with Twizell driving. Like me, he was in country clothes now—jeans, boots, windbreaker—except that his were new. I wondered where the money for the clothes, the squash gear, rent for the serviced apartment and the car had come from. I didn't ask, I had a feeling he'd lie. But it was something to think about.

The route was north-west and the distance about a hundred kilometres. We rolled through the Newcastle suburbs into the lush Hunter Valley country where they can pursue almost any agricultural and pastoral activity. The web had told me that the area had been hard hit by the floods of the year before and I could see some signs—dead grass woven into wire fences, fresh paint on new fence rails and deep gullies in paddocks where flash floods had run through.

He turned on the radio and we heard the news about the killing of Osama Bin Laden. We listened in silence to the long report.

When it finished Twizell said, 'Raghead bastard. Good riddance. What do you reckon?'

'I'm not sorry he's dead, but I don't much like the sound of the way they went about it.'

'Only way, mate.'

'What would you know?'

He laughed. 'I've done a bit.'

'Where? When?'

'Best forgotten.'

That made another thing I didn't know about him. It was an uncomfortable feeling. He was a volatile type, a mood switcher. I reminded myself not to take him lightly.

Vineyards and a township and then we were in scrubby country and on the upslope. The range ahead was blue in the distance and took on the typical grey-green colour of the bush the closer we got. We left the tarmac for a dirt road that had been reasonably graded and gave the big 4WD a smooth ride. Then it was off on a rougher road and onto what was really just a track through sparsely wooded country cut by a succession of shallow streams, some of them little more than linked puddles. Twizell enjoyed splashing through them and using the squirter to clean the windscreen.

'Way to go,' he said. 'When we came here last it was in an old ute. Jolted us and I got bogged once. What are you doing?'

I'd hit the window button and was staring out. 'Trying to see if any vehicle has passed by recently. What do you think?'

'I'm no bushman, mate. The bush is just somewhere for me to have fun in. Get me underground and I can read the signs like an Apache; up here I'm just a tourist.'

I wasn't a bushman either, but I fancied I could see tyre tracks in spots and there was a sheen of oil in one of the ruts made by a vehicle spinning its wheels after crossing a stream. It looked fresh. The climb got steeper and then levelled out.

Twizell pointed to some rusted machinery on a concrete slab, all overgrown by creeper. 'Used to be an army training camp of some sort out here. Fair bit of equipment left behind the way they do. Wasteful buggers. The cottage was for the caretaker. All gone now.'

'How far to go?'

'About one k.'

'Stop. We don't want to advertise ourselves.'

'Why not? Oh, Kristie's tough guy. You're scared of him, aren't you?'

'No, Jack, I feel the same way about him as I do about you.'

He stopped the car and worked his shoulders loosely. 'And how's that?'

I hadn't formulated it fully but I did now. 'I don't trust him and I don't want him to get the jump on me.'

'Fair enough,' he said. 'I feel just like that about you.'

I nodded. Always good to know where you stand.

'Give me the keys,' I said.

'What?'

'Jack, you're the chauffeur and guide on this trip, but you're not the boss. Give me the keys.'

'Fuck you,' he said, but he tossed me the keys and I locked the Patrol and pocketed them.

'Got your gun?'

'Don't worry about it,' I said.

'Anyone who doesn't worry about guns is an idiot.'

'You're right there.'

19

We walked along the track keeping as quiet as we could, although I doubted we'd be walking into serious danger. After a while Twizell gestured to me and I followed him into a clearing roughly the size of a tennis court. The area had been excavated but not levelled, and it had been scoured by the flood. The surface was rocky with boulders sticking up here and there. At the end of the clearing a huge rock jutted up abruptly. The face looked smooth in spots and, while it wasn't anything like fifty metres to the top, it was high enough and I'd have said impossible to climb.

'That's the fucker,' Twizell said. 'A cunt of a climb. I pity those poor bastards of army trainees who probably had to go up it before breakfast, lunch and dinner.'

'Did Kristie climb it?'

He laughed. 'She tried. Got stuck two-thirds of the way there. I had to go up and around and throw her a rope.'

'Game of her to try.'

'She was game all right, and a very good root.'

We rejoined the track and moved forward. Twizell kept to the edge and the tree cover and I followed. I had the .38 in a shoulder holster under the denim vest I was wearing and I hoped it'd stay there, warm and cosy. Twizell was enjoying himself and exaggerated his watchful movements as we drew closer to where he said the cottage was. Still, he seemed to know the rudiments of a covert approach. He pulled back under the branches of a spreading eucalypt and pointed.

'The cottage is just around this last bend. What do you want to do?'

'Stop playing Hollywood heroes and go and see if they're there.'

'You're no fun.'

A helicopter passed over and Twizell looked thoughtful. 'Probably interested in chop-chop out here. They hide it in vineyards. Nice business to be in if you've got the protection.'

'Business at hand, Jack,' I said, 'not your entrepreneurial future.'

We rounded the bend and walked into a large clearing in front of a green-painted fibro cottage with a brick chimney. I was reminded of the derelict Tanner house at Dudley, except that this showed signs of constant maintenance— weeds slashed, cement paths swept and windows intact. A big white SUV stood near the cottage with its rear hatch wide open.

'Nice wheels,' Twizell said. 'Kristie's riding high.'

We walked towards the cottage.

'What does this guy do?' Twizell asked.

I didn't reply.

The cottage door opened and Templeton stepped outside.

'One of the things he does,' I said, 'is stay alert and we'd better do the same.'

I raised a hand. 'Gidday, Rod.'

'Hardy,' he said. 'And this must be Johnnie Twizell.'

'Jack,' Twizell said. He moved forward and stuck out his hand. I could tell he was measuring Templeton for height, weight and capability. At that point I would've put my money on Rod, but Jack was tricky.

Templeton shook his hand casually while looking at me, evaluating. 'Come to see Kristie, Hardy?'

'That's right.'

Templeton was wearing cord trousers, boots and a flannie over a Newcastle Knights T-shirt. He hadn't shaved for a few days but his eyes were clear and he had the look you saw in some boxers, like Ali, and some AFL players, like James Hird—perfect balance. 'How about you, Jack?'

Twizell shrugged but I judged that he'd wisely decided he'd be over-matched against Templeton. 'Along for the ride. Just showing Hardy the way. Is Kristie here?'

'She is. Are you hoping to make amends for what you did to her?'

'Maybe just explain.'

'Fair enough. C'mon on in.'

The door led straight into a large living room with poor lighting, a threadbare carpet and furniture that looked as though it had been scavenged from the back lanes of Newtown. Through the gloom I saw a passage leading to other rooms. It was a fair bet that the kitchen would have a wood stove—the era was right and the air had the right smell.

Templeton invited us to sit down and said he'd fetch Kristie.

'Place has a certain charm,' I said.

Twizell pointed to the fireplace. 'Gets fucking cold in winter. You need that. I nearly did my back in chopping wood.'

'You're nervous, Jack.'

'Something about that guy worries me.'

Something about the time Templeton was taking worried me. I heard activity outside near the SUV and wondered for a minute whether they were going to take off. But no engine started. Then I heard voices raised and a slap. I got to my feet just as Templeton came back pulling Kristie with him by the arm. She was a big, strong woman but he managed her easily with one hand. In his other hand he had a double-barrel shotgun with the stock cut down to a pistol-grip size. He was wearing the leather jacket I'd first seen him in and his face was set in hard, determined lines. He almost threw Kristie into a chair.

He pointed the shottie at Twizell but I could tell he had me well within his field of vision. He said, 'Stay where you are, Hardy. Don't move a muscle.' He gestured at Twizell.

'Get up. You're coming with me.'

'The fuck I am.'

Two long strides took Templeton across to where Twizell was pressed back in his chair. He hit him hard with a backhander, grabbed the collar of his jacket and pulled him to his feet as though he weighed nothing. He rammed the short barrels up under Twizell's ear and dragged him towards the door.

'Make a move, Hardy, and it's one barrel for him and one for you, or her.'

I froze. Kristie screamed something and Twizell yelled as the sharp, sawn metal tore into his skin. Then Templeton had him at the door.

'Open it!'

Blood was running down Twizell's neck and his eyes were wide in terror. He opened the door. Templeton tapped him on the sweet spot just above the temple and Twizell sagged. In almost the same movement Templeton hoisted him onto his shoulder with the shottie now pointed at me. He backed through the door. I pulled out the .38, jumped up and went after him. A sawn-off shotgun has spread but no range and I thought I might get a chance for a shot when his gun was ineffective. But Templeton was extraordinarily quick. He'd thrown Twizell into the back of the SUV and extended his long arm out over the car as I reached the door. He fired, I ducked, and the pellets splattered against the wall of the cottage and ricocheted around me.

The engine roared, the wheels spun, and the SUV rocketed, swerving, across the clearing and down the track.

20

I stood, staring at nothing. Templeton's action, brutal, super-efficient, utterly surprising, had stunned me. In the cottage, Kristie was hysterical, throwing herself around the room, wailing and tearing at her hair like a berserker. She launched herself at me and beat on my chest with her fists.

'Why didn't you shoot him? He doesn't love me.'

She was fit and strong and in her passion her blows hurt. I pushed her off and held her at a distance as she flailed at me, crying and snarling. All you can do is wait for the moment to pass. It took a long time. Eventually she calmed down. We went through to the kitchen at the back of the cottage. Sure enough, there was a wood stove and a kerosene fridge. I found a bottle of brandy on a sideboard and Coca-Cola and ice in the fridge and made her a drink. I took my brandy straight. We sat at the vinyl-topped table with our drinks.

'Have you got any pills?' she asked.

'What kind of pills?'

'Any kind.'

'No.'

'Shit, I'm going to need something to get through this. My dad's dead and my brother did it and my other brother . . . And fucking Rod . . . '

'Sorry, no pills. You seemed to be coping.'

She laughed, lifted her glass. 'With this, and love. What I thought was love.'

We sat quietly for a while and had more brandy. The bathroom was in a lean-to at the back of the building. She went there and came back with her face repaired. Her heavy makeup had smeared and smudged. She'd restored it expertly and regained her composure. With her height and heavy features, she looked a little like Angelica Huston in certain roles. She'd had some experience at recovering from bad times and she was putting it to use now.

'You'd better tell me all about it,' I said.

'I'd better make some coffee and something to eat or I'm going to be too pissed to think. Why didn't you go after him?'

'We left the car a kilometre down the track.'

She nodded and set about brewing coffee—loading the percolator, pushing kindling and paper into the stove, watching while it caught and adding bigger pieces of split wood. She was wearing tight jeans, low-heeled boots and a dark, long-sleeved top. Her movements were decisive and deft. She stopped from time to time, presumably remembering happier moments, but she kept working.

I had my mobile sitting on the table along with the .38. The phone rang. I felt sure I knew who it'd be. I answered.

'Hardy.'

'This is Rod. Is Kristie okay?'

'Sort of.'

'Tell her I'm sorry.'

'Tell her yourself.'

'No.'

'Where are you?'

He laughed. 'Goodbye, Hardy. I hope never to see you again.'

'Don't count on it. How's Jack?'

He cut the call.

Kristie looked up from what she was doing and wiped her hands on a cloth. Hung the cloth where it belonged. Normal things. She knew how to cope.

'That him? What did he say?'

'He said he was sorry.'

She shook her head. 'He's not, but he will be.'

Kristie made the coffee and we drank it spiked with the brandy. She stuffed rocket and grated cheese into some bread rolls and I ate three to her one. She told me that Templeton had said he was due some leave and that they should get away somewhere. She'd suggested the cottage.

'And you wanted to put him to the test?'

'Johnnie told you about that, did he? Yeah, well I did. I was very keen on him and I wouldn't have cared if he didn't make it.'

'Did he?'

She paused and drank some coffee. 'He went up it like climbing a ladder. Then we . . . well, what does it matter now? I know why he kept me with him. I should have known from other clues.'

She said that when he'd had too much to drink, Templeton let slip that he was unhappy in the police force. He also talked about the buried money more often than she was comfortable with.

'Rog . . . Rod, that is, knew that you wanted to talk to me because I told him. And he knew that you'd be in touch with Johnnie. Johnnie knew that I'd bring a new man here. He just used me as bait to get hold of Johnnie. He's a bloody good actor. I believed what he told me about . . .'

'The undercover guys have to be that,' I said. 'It might not have been acting, altogether. He sounded sincere when he said he was sorry.'

'No.' She touched her face. 'Looking like this puts blokes off, all except the kinky ones and who needs them? Fuck him!'

What she said about Templeton's actions made sense and fitted in with a hint Ted Power had given me: *I don't think he feels fully appreciated.* Kristie was constructing defences, something she was good at. I suspected she might be in the mood to be useful to Marisha and I could do myself some good by bringing them together.

'He'll make Johnnie show him where the money is,' Kristie said. 'He'll get it, kill Johnnie and disappear.'

'To do all that's a big ask. Twizell's tough and he's been around.'

'Johnnie's not tough. He only acts tough.'

'He implied he'd had military experience.'

'Yeah, in some bullshit peace-keeping gig. Briefly.'

I wasn't sure peace-keeping operations were as soft as she thought. Maybe Jack Twizell could make a stand, but I couldn't see any way I could play a part in that. I tried to tell myself I was in the box seat—Kristie could tell all she knew about the Twizell family papers and I could complete my job for Wakefield. Whether he got what he wanted or not I'd be paid. And there was Marisha. But there was also Hector Tanner, who couldn't be feeling well disposed towards me, and I had a guilty feeling about having led Jack Twizell into a potentially deadly trap. Things are never simple.

Kristie was listless, a bit drunk from the brandy and at a low ebb. She needed activity and motivation.

'Come on, Kristie,' I said. 'We have to get out of here. There's someone I want you to talk to and I need to ask you about Grandma Twizell's papers when you're up to it.'

She nodded and stood. 'I'll get my stuff.'

'Let's hope Rod didn't disable Jack's car.'

He hadn't. He was banking on us not knowing where Jack's cave was. Safe enough for me, but I didn't know about Kristie. She'd brought all she wanted to take from the cottage in a backpack. I unlocked the car and we climbed in.

'This is Johnnie's?' she said.

I nodded.

'I wonder where he got the money.'

'I do, too.'

'How long after he got out before you caught up with him?'

'Day and a bit.'

'Long enough for him to do a deal with someone else about getting the money and getting something in advance. He'd have been thinking about it from day one, inside.'

I'd had a similar thought myself, but then I wasn't worried about the money. It loomed as more important now and Marisha'd want to know the outcome, if any. I started the car and got moving. I'd had a fair amount of brandy but I'd blotted it up with the bread and cheese and there was still a way to go before any chance of being breathalysed. I felt clear-headed, but Kristie had been through the wringer; she fell asleep and snored.

She woke up when we hit the paved road.

'Did I snore?'

'You did.'

'Ever since those bloody operations. What now?'

It seemed to be as good a time as any. 'Do you know where Twizell buried the money?'

She laughed. 'Not a clue.'

'Did Templeton ask you?'

'I don't want to talk about him. I did a flit from my flat, owing rent, and chucked my shitty job. I missed Dad's funeral because of that bastard and now I've got nowhere to go. Shit I'm a mess.'

'I've got a friend . . .'

'You've got a friend? That surprises me. You're a hard case.'

'You'd know. Anyway, she's a tough nut, too. She's a journalist working on a book about your family. She'd like to talk to you. She had the inside running with Jobe until Joseph . . .'

I let her sit for a while. She stared out the window as if she was reviewing her life from who knows when to that point. 'Okay, okay,' she said. 'Why not? The things I could tell her.'

'She won't pay you, but she'd put you up for a bit, give you some breathing space.'

I drove through the suburbs, careful not to attract any attention. I was probably still over the limit and a booking for DUI was a complication I didn't need. Kristie was silent, picking at the flaking paint on her fingernails. She had a lot to think about—a dead father, a brother in gaol and one on the loose; two ex-lovers and a lot of money. What I wanted her to think about was the Twizell papers, but they seemed secondary to everything else.

I headed towards Redcliff but pulled over.

'What?' Kristie said.

'I'm calling Marisha.'

'*Marisha.* Bloody pretentious name. Where does it come from?'

You have to know when to just let the talk flow. 'I don't know,' I said. 'Could be Russian.'

'Remember when everyone was all worried about Russia?'

'I do.'

'Before my time. Were you worried?'

'I was just as worried about the Yanks.'

'Are you worried about the Muslims now?'

'Not especially.'

'Why not?'

'They're divided among themselves, I think. They'll squabble.'

'I haven't heard that.'

'People are saying it. It's not original.'

Cars passed us as we stood with the wheels just out of the drainage gutter. A hoon with his radio blaring broke her pensive mood.

'You know how to talk to people, don't you?'

I shrugged. 'It's what I do—talk, and listen.'

'You really want to know about old Granny Twizell's papers, don't you?'

'Yes.'

She smiled. 'You scratch my back and I'll scratch yours.'

21

Marisha was at home and hard at work but she was happy to be interrupted to meet Kristie. The two women circled each other warily. When Kristie indicated her willingness to be interviewed and to comment on some of the material Marisha had assembled, things went better. There was a small sunroom off the living room which Marisha used for storage, but it contained a divan and they arranged for Kristie to sleep there for a few nights while they did their business and she worked out what she wanted to do next.

But I had business of my own with Kristie and when Marisha went out to buy some supplies I tackled her.

'You were going to tell me more about the Twizell family papers when you got the news about Jobe. I want to hear what you have to say. It's what I came up here to work on before things took the turn they did.'

'I'd just about forgotten that.'

'I hope you haven't forgotten where they are.'

'It's a funny thing; I was quite prepared to go on disliking you but you're really a nice bloke under all the can-do stuff, aren't you?'

I shrugged. 'Hope so.'

'I'd be interested, except that you're hot for Marisha, right?'

'Yes, with reservations.'

She sighed. 'Story of my life. Missing out on right blokes and taking on wrong ones. I've moved around a lot in the last few years after coming out of hospital. Short-term rentals and sub-lets. Had to go back into hospital a few times. I didn't want to haul a lot of stuff around with me. I've got a rented storage locker in town. When Granny Twizell died I was sort of unofficial executor. I helped cleaning out her stuff. Hec and Joseph weren't interested. I took most of it to Vinnies and the Smith Family but I kept those papers, as you call them. They're in storage along with some of my clothes and books and uni notes and like that.'

'Will you let me look at them?'

'Sure. Didn't you say there could be a dollar in it? Give me a day to settle in here and see how things go with your girlfriend and I'll take you to them.'

I phoned Wakefield with the possibly good news.

'That's marvellous. Well done.'

'We don't know that they're what you want yet.'

'From what you say there's a good chance. I'll drive up tomorrow. I take it Ms Tanner won't object to me being present?'

'I think she'll be delighted.'

'Good. I hope you're staying clear of all that messy business with the other Tanners.'

'Not exactly.'

'What about Twizell? Is he involved at this point?'

I didn't want to go into that with him and gave a vague answer. There was excitement in his voice and he mentioned a bonus. All in all, a very satisfactory phone call.

Kristie said her car was out of action and asked if she could use Jack's.

'Not a good idea,' I said. 'If Jack did some sort of deal with people about the money and they financed him into the 4WD they'll be on the lookout for it when he doesn't show up.'

She nodded. 'I'll need some money to get my car out of hock.'

I didn't want her running around freely just yet. I told her the man backing my investigation was coming up to look at the papers and that if they proved to be what he hoped, I was sure he'd give her some money.

'That raises the stakes,' she said. 'What're you going to do now?'

'Leave the Patrol somewhere, go back to my motel and wait for your call tomorrow.'

'What about Johnnie and Rod?'

'Don't worry about it. Work with Marisha and see what happens about the papers. A new start.'

'Who's this client of yours?'

'Professor Henry Wakefield.'

'Is he a spunk?'

I laughed. 'You're recovering fast. I'm off. Tell Marisha I'll be in touch.'

'I bet you will.'

I drove back to the CBD, left the Patrol in a parking station and handed the keys in to the attendant. If it ran up an overdue bill that wasn't my problem. Twizell's abduction *was* my problem, sort of, and I decided I had to come clean about it. I phoned Kerry Watson and arranged to meet him at a pub near my motel. He arrived fifteen minutes after the appointed time, tired and in a bad mood. He flopped down in a chair at the table I'd picked and looked at me with bleary eyes.

'I've had a shitty day,' he said. 'Are you going to improve my mood?'

'I'll buy you a drink, a couple maybe.'

'That's a good start. Double scotch and something to munch.'

I wasn't planning to do any more driving so I ordered two doubles and bought a packet of crisps and one of nuts. Watson didn't bother with the preliminaries. He took a swig and split the packets open with his big, blunt fingers. He munched a fistful of both and washed them down with more whisky.

'Did you ever see *In the Heat of the Night*?' he said.

'Of course. Great picture.'

'Remember what Steiger says when he answers the phone?'

'"Talk to me."'

'Right.'

I told him everything he needed to know—about my and Twizell's encounter with Hector and Clem, about Twizell and the money, about Kristie and Rod Templeton, about me falling into the trap of Kristie being the bait and about Templeton's grabbing of Twizell with the money as his object.

Watson ate and drank and said nothing. When I'd finished he pushed his glass at me and I got him a refill.

He sipped, cautiously. 'You should've told me you'd met up with Hector.'

'I had no idea where he'd go.'

'Then you and Twizell hare off to find the sister and this is all about something you haven't explained.'

'It's separate. It's non-criminal.'

'Everything's criminal, Hardy, with the Tanners concerned and with you, I suspect.'

'Hector said he had places to go to that no one knew about. I asked Kristie if she knew about them and she said no.'

'Do you believe her?'

'I think so.'

'You *think*. Okay.' He took his notebook out. 'Rego number of the 4WD this Templeton took off in?'

'I didn't notice.'

'Great help. What else do you know about him?'

'Not much. He used the name Roger Tarrant when he was working for the Tanners.'

I knew more, but I'd leave Watson to find that out for himself from internal sources.

Looking disgusted, he scribbled a few notes. 'No idea where to look for him?'

'Where there's caves.'

'Fucking caves everywhere.'

'Twizell's a local boy.'

He put the notebook away. 'Thanks a lot, Hardy. Just what I need. You've given me a rogue cop and someone under duress who's going to be forced to violate his parole and no idea where to find them. Plus Hector Tanner out in the wind with a heavy who's prepared to do nasty things with a bolt-cutter.'

'Sorry.'

'So you're just opting out and getting on with your own cosy little business?'

'I hope so.'

He got up and finished off his drink. 'I doubt it. You're at the Maritime, right?'

'Yes.'

'Thanks for the drinks. Stay there. You'll be hearing from us.'

He walked out, moving very steadily the way you do when you have a heavy, but not too heavy, load on.

I went back to the motel, checked Twizell out and tried not to think about him. I couldn't help thinking about Templeton, weighing him up the way Twizell had. I had a score to settle with him from back when I didn't know he was a cop and I felt I owed him something more now. It was only luck that I hadn't caught some of the shotgun pellets and it only takes one in the right spot to do a lot of damage.

I tried to put myself in his shoes and, as I sifted through the things he'd done, I knew what I'd be worried about—certainly Hector Tanner, the police service he'd deserted and possibly the people who'd stolen the buried money in the first place. And the difficulty of recovering it if Twizell talked, as he probably would. He might have to use Twizell and if he did, the odds might shift.

I'd had enough to drink and had no interest in food. A motel room can be one of the loneliest places in the world. I watched the news on television but my interest in the royal wedding was less than zero and it seemed to be blotting everything else out except the death of Bin Laden. Pakistan was getting shitty about it, but an American commentator made the point that it had probably assured Obama of another term.

'Is that why he did it?' the interviewer asked.

'Look,' the commentator said, 'he took a big risk and it came off. The American people like that.'

'What? Taking a risk?'

'No, the risk coming off. That's seen as leadership.'

'Is it?'

'You tell me.'

I picked up *Lord Jim* and lost myself in it for an hour. I'd set myself to read some of the classics—Conrad, Hardy, Trollope—and I'd been doing it with pleasure for a while. Couldn't come at Henry James, no matter how hard I tried. I was jerked out of the nineteenth century and the jungle and all the moral dilemmas by my mobile.

'Cliff, you bastard, it's Marisha. Why'd you take off like that?'

'Things to do. Knackered after a hard day, and I wanted to let you and Kristie get acquainted and get to work. How's it going?'

'Oh, right, change of subject. Cliff deftly avoids emotional difficulty. Lily told me about that. Well . . . pretty good. I'm out on the balcony now and she's having a shower so I can talk. She's cagey but she's given me some good stuff and I'm sure there's more to come. It's one of those times when you get on to something and realise you couldn't have done without it. Know what I mean?'

'I do. That's good. I'm hoping she's going to take me to the documents my client's interested in tomorrow.'

'Okay. What about Twizell and the cop and the buried money?'

'Like I said, I'm not so interested in all that.'

'Bullshit. You're interested and so am I.'

'You're right.'

'I wish you were here. I'd like to fuck you, but I guess it'll keep. I'll be seeing you tomorrow?'

'You will.'

'You sure?'

'I'm sure.'

'Goodnight, Cliff.'

She put a lot into that, but I was beginning to realise that Marisha put a lot into everything and you never knew what really mattered to her and what didn't matter quite so much.

22

Watson summoned me to the police station and I made a full statement of my dealings with Hector and Joseph Tanner, my meetings with Twizell and the encounter with Templeton. They recorded it on video and provided a transcript. I signed it. I handed in Hector's Beretta. Nothing pleased them and I didn't expect otherwise. I was instructed to contact the police immediately if I heard from Hector, Twizell or Templeton and threatened with prosecution if I didn't.

There was a message from Wakefield at the motel. I phoned Marisha's number and spoke to Kristie. She said she'd take us to her storage locker. I phoned Wakefield. He arrived in his Mercedes and we picked up Kristie. I told Marisha I'd be back after this bit of business.

'For a celebration?' she said.

'We'll see.'

Kristie was impressed by well-groomed Wakefield in his

suit and behind the leather-padded wheel of his Merc. She rode up front with him. We drove to Broadmeadow to a concrete yard enclosed by a cyclone-wire fence. It housed about fifty lockable sheds ranging from the size of three-car garages to ones like Kristie's, not bigger than a decent-sized garden shed. God knows what secret and illicit things were inside the sheds. Kristie had a key to the gate and we drove in and parked beside her spot. She unlocked the door and stepped aside.

'I haven't been here for a while. It'll be musty.'

'What did you do with the stuff from your flat?' I said.

'I told you, I did a flit. I dumped it. I thought I was starting a new life and here I am, back with the old stuff.'

'It could still be a new beginning for you,' Wakefield said, 'if what's here is what I'm looking for.'

I started to move some cardboard boxes. 'How's that, Henry?'

'Well, I'm thinking about a book and a film and selling the manuscript itself. It could amount to quite a lot of money and Kristine and I would have a contract.'

That surprised me. I hadn't thought Wakefield was the sharing kind, but he had seemed to find a quick rapport with Kristie. He took off his suit jacket, tucked his silk tie inside his jacket and rolled up his sleeves.

'Now, what are we looking for?' he said.

'A trunk, a sort of sea chest,' Kristie said.

'Of course.'

We moved boxes and large Chinese zipped laundry bags until we reached the chest. It was a small version—more like a woman's travelling trunk than a sea chest, but it had faded stickers on it and was tied around with rope. Wakefield picked it up almost reverently and carried it out into the light.

'Fingers crossed,' I said. I offered my Swiss army knife but Wakefield insisted on untying the knots. Then he stood back and invited Kristie to open the trunk. Impeccable manners.

Kristie squatted, undid the clasp and lifted the lid. She took out some letters tied with faded ribbon and then a heavy object wrapped in brown paper.

'This is it.'

She eased the paper away to reveal the black, gold-embossed cover of a large Bible. Most of the pages had gone and the covers were used to protect and keep together some more letters, some photographs and a stained, bound notebook, quarto-sized. She presented it like a votive offering to Wakefield, who held up one finger.

'Just a minute.'

He put the notebook on the concrete and took a pair of surgical gloves from his suit jacket. He pulled them on and opened the notebook. He turned several of the closely written, yellowed pages carefully. He closed the notebook.

'My God,' he said softly. 'It's the journal of William Dalgarno Twizell.'

I didn't know whether the courtly gesture was an act or whether it came naturally to him, but he took big Kristie

Tanner in his arms as if she was a fragile ballerina and kissed her on both cheeks. She liked it.

Wakefield insisted on stopping to buy champagne on the way back to Marisha's flat. Kristie sat with the little trunk on her lap and kept stroking the faded, peeling surface.

'How did you hear about it, Henry?' Kristie asked.

Henry now, I thought.

'Diligent research,' he said.

By whom? I wondered.

Wakefield explained that there had been occasional mentions of the Twizell papers in Hunter Valley newspapers in the late nineteenth century and again later when there was a family dispute over land.

'Just a hint,' he said. 'Just a clue, but with a lot of hard work and a little luck nuggets can be found. By the way, thank you, Cliff. You've done superbly well.'

I doubt Jack Twizell would agree, I thought, but I didn't say anything. All jobs have rough edges.

It was 1pm when we got back to Marisha's place and we had a party. Marisha was happy with her morning's work and she cheerfully went domestic, laying out biscuits, pate and cheese as we cracked Wakefield's expensive champagne.

'No flutes?' he asked Marisha as she got out glasses.

'Don't believe in them. Too small.'

He laughed. 'You've got a point.' He poured the glasses

full, spilling some. He put his arm around Kristie's broad shoulders. 'Kristie—to you!'

'Are you sure the journal's genuine?' I asked.

'I'll have to have it thoroughly authenticated, of course, but I'm pretty confident.'

'What about the letters and other stuff?'

'Playing devil's advocate, Cliff?'

'Someone has to.'

'You're right.' Pulling on another set of gloves, Wakefield took the papers from the trunk, handling them very carefully. He unfolded one and swore when flakes of it fell away. 'This isn't the time or the place. As I say, I'm confident there's a remarkable story to be told.'

He smiled at Kristie as he replaced the papers, putting the yellowed flakes inside on the gloves and restoring everything to the trunk. Then he picked up his glass and took a swig.

Wakefield relaxed his academic manner after a few drinks and told some good stories about his students and colleagues. He took off his tie and seemed to get younger with the wine and with basking in Kristie's admiration. She drank her share and was the most at ease I'd seen her. When Marisha slyly took advantage of this and slipped in a few questions, Kristie responded with some information about the Tanner enterprise that opened Marisha's eyes. Tipping me the wink, she slipped away to make some notes.

We had Van Morrison on the stereo and Wakefield

surprised us all by singing pretty good harmony with him—
not easy to do.

Marisha came back and we partied on. After a while, with
a considerable buzz on, Marisha and I went for a walk on
the beach. We took off our shoes, rolled up our pants and
splashed along in the cold shallows.

'Things seem to be working out pretty well, Cliff,' Marisha
said.

I grabbed her and kissed her. 'I'd say so. Are we past our
little . . . emotional difficulty?'

'Yeah, let's hope we have some more.'

'Bound to.'

We walked in companionable silence until the wind got
colder and we agreed it was time for coffee. When we
got back to the flat we found that Wakefield, Kristie and her
belongings, and the Twizell papers and the trunk had gone.

Marisha and I tidied the flat, stacked the dishwasher and
went to bed. We surfaced in the early evening and turned on
the television news. After the usual political lies and gossip
there was a report of a car crash on the highway south of
Newcastle. A Mercedes sedan carrying a man and a woman
had collided with a petrol tanker. The tanker driver was
unhurt, but the car and its occupants were incinerated. The
car was identified as having belonged to Professor Henry
Wakefield of the Independent University.

part three

23

The university turned on an elaborate funeral service for Wakefield. I didn't go. Our relationship had improved over the time I'd known him but that was as far as my feelings for him went. His death brought home to me again the fragility of life. You take your pills, do your exercises, watch what you eat and drink, and a faulty tyre or a patch of oil on a road can make it all meaningless.

I stayed in Newcastle for Kristie's funeral and to comfort Marisha, who took the death hard. She'd lost a valuable informant, but also someone she'd come to like and admire in the short time they'd had together.

'She'd been through a lot,' Marisha said as we stood in the rain at the cemetery, 'and she was still in there pitching.' I agreed.

The day was cold, grey and wet the way it should be for a funeral. It was a big affair and the second in a short space of time for the Tanners and their many connections.

There was a heavy police presence on the lookout for Hector but he didn't show. Joseph, who'd been indicted and was awaiting trial, was allowed to attend. He was closely guarded but not under restraint. He saw me and scowled, or perhaps he was scowling at Marisha. Anyway, he didn't hold the expression long. There were a lot of cameras around and he didn't want to look too threatening on the front page of the *Newcastle Herald*.

We didn't go to the wake. Without saying so we were both aware that the last wake we'd been at was Lily's and that, with all due regard to the love we'd had for her, was something we wanted to put behind us.

Kerry Watson fronted up as we were leaving the cemetery. He looked as worn out as ever.

'Going to the booze-up?'

'No,' I said.

He nodded. 'Duty calls, but the Tanners have given me a lot of grief over the years. I'll be glad to get a drink out of them.'

'Nothing on Templeton and Twizell?' I said.

'To tell you the truth, we've been too busy with other things to bother much. See you, Hardy, Ms Henderson.'

There hadn't been a lot to say about the documents lost in Wakefield's car. Whether the journal he'd found was real or a fake, or whether it was supported or not by the letters and other papers, no one would ever know. The story of the *Dunbar* would remain as it was.

Marisha was quiet on the drive back to her flat. We hadn't spoken about it but we both knew I'd be heading back to Sydney soon. We'd been getting along very well and, in the way that people do when they find mental and sexual compatibility, we each had a good idea what the other was thinking about.

'Come on,' I said, 'there's something on your mind about Templeton and Jack Twizell, right?'

'Mmm.'

'What?'

'You're not interested in following it up, are you?'

'No, not much.'

'Because there's no money in it?'

'Partly.'

'What if there was?'

'Are you offering to pay me again?'

She touched my arm. 'No, I don't think either of us'd like that much, and I couldn't afford you for very long.'

'What is it, then?'

'Let me think about it.'

We got back to the flat, hung up our wet coats and agreed we should have a drink for Kristie. Marisha got out the vodka that was Kristie's favourite tipple and built two big ones with tonic and ice and slices of lime. We stood by the window looking out at the grey, misty view, and touched glasses.

'Kristie!'

We drank.

'Hector Tanner,' Marisha said suddenly.

'Jesus Christ, are you having dealings with him? He's bloody dangerous. How did you contact him?'

'He contacted me. I have to admit it was scary. He rang me and it was clear he knew a lot about me and what I was doing. I nearly pissed myself but all he wanted was to help me.'

'I can't believe I'm hearing this. All Hector Tanner would ever want to do is help himself.'

'You're wrong. Listen to me. He's not as bad as Joseph, not really. Don't forget I got a lot of stuff from Jobe and Kristie. Hector never killed anyone. He was more of an organiser, an administrator, if you will.'

'You're kidding yourself.'

'Maybe, and I'm being super-cautious.'

'You better be. How long has this been going on?'

Her laugh was unlike her usual full-bodied guffaw, more uncertain. 'Just since yesterday.'

'What're you hoping to get from him?'

'Whatever I can. More to the point is what he wants from me.'

'And that is?'

'He wants help from you.'

'From me?'

'Yes, he's been in touch with Templeton, who he calls Tarrant, but same bloke. Templeton says Twizell won't tell him where the money is.'

'Oh, so he wants Hector to come along with Clem and the bolt-cutters.'

'No. According to Hector, Twizell says he knows he'll be killed if he tells Templeton what he wants so he doesn't care what Templeton or anyone else does to him. He wants to negotiate a safe passage and wants you to supervise the deal. Broker it, as it were.'

'That's crazy. Why would I do that?'

'Twizell trusts you and Hector and Templeton respect you.'

'You're snowing me.'

'No. That's what they say and I believe it. Anyway, they thought the proposition'd have a better chance with you coming from me.'

'Who thought that?'

She shrugged. 'Your guess is as good as mine.'

I'd been so astonished by this that I'd neglected my drink. The ice had melted. I took a long swig and Marisha did the same.

'Ever feel manipulated?' I said.

'Manipulated and manipulating—I'm a journalist.'

And maybe that's all you are, I thought, but I didn't say so. Marisha took her drink into her study. I paced around as the light dimmed outside and the air cooled in the room. In the few days since Wakefield and Kristie had left I'd stayed in the flat and had got used to its workings. But I'd left Marisha alone to write while I checked my emails, rang Megan, did

215

things. We hadn't been in each other's pockets. Plenty of chances for her to contact people and be contacted. Hector Tanner and who else?

I finished the drink and resisted the urge to have another. I needed a clear head for thinking. One thought was a repeat of what I'd had a couple of times before—Jack Twizell was a smart cookie and a game one. No comfort there—in my experience smart, brave men are usually at their smartest and bravest when they're looking out for themselves.

Then I had another thought. What if Templeton wasn't a rogue cop after all? What if all this was an act to get hold of Hector Tanner and clear up a nagging rumour about a lot of missing money? And resolve what had happened to a British backpacker?

Marisha came out of her study long enough to give me Templeton's mobile number—different from the one I already had and which hadn't answered the last few times I'd tried it.

'Going to ring him?'

I nodded.

'Good.' She went back to work.

I knew what an upright citizen *should* do—go to Watson and have him set up the system they use to locate the source of mobile phone calls. Why didn't I do it? Partly out of respect for Templeton's intelligence and resources. For all I knew there were ways someone could know he was being tracked and Templeton might have sources still within the police force to keep him informed of what was being done to catch him. I couldn't see a pair like Templeton and Tanner positioning themselves where a police raid would be effective.

I punched in the numbers.

'This is Hardy.'

'Just you?'

'Just me.'

'Where are you?'

'Why?'

'Just answer the question.'

'No, we're not going to play it that way. If you've got someone watching me, have him come in and I'll give him a drink.'

Templeton laughed. 'Okay. Your girlfriend's put you in the picture, has she?'

'Just barely. Speaking of girlfriends, I suppose you were sorry to hear that Kristie burned to death.'

There was a pause before he came back on the line. 'You want to make this hard or easy?'

'I don't want it at all, but I feel partly responsible for Jack Twizell being in the shit and I've got scores to settle with you and Hector.'

'This isn't about settling scores. It's about money.'

'If you say so.'

'I do. All you have to do is exactly what you're told and

everything will go smoothly. Twizell walks away, Hector and I take the money and you get on with whatever. Oh, and your girlfriend writes her book.'

It's a funny thing, but as he spoke these words I knew it was never going to be anything like that. I didn't know why, but I knew. The reference to Marisha was a sort of clue that the net was spread wider than he wanted me to believe.

'This is the deal,' Templeton said. 'We meet up on the highway and go north up the coast. That's all Twizell will say at this point.'

'Terrific. How *is* Jack? Rough him up much?'

'No, he has to stay fit. He's got work to do. One other thing—you're going into the cave with him.'

'I'm claustrophobic.'

'Too bad. That's our condition. You bring him and the money out. I don't want him disappearing into a cave system and coming out somewhere west of Woop Woop.'

'What's to stop you and Hector bumping us off there and then?'

'We won't. We're not killers.'

'Just thieves.'

'That's right.'

'Are you finding Hector useful?'

'He will be when we need to launder the money.'

'What if I bring the police along?'

'We'd know.'

'What if I do nothing?'

'If that happens, your girlfriend'll never write her book. I wouldn't hurt her but I guarantee you every note she's taken, every tape she's recorded, every photo, will go up in smoke and it'll be all your fault. Happy to live with that? This is a clean operation, Hardy. Win, win all around.'

'With a lot of trust involved.'

'Some, yes.'

'I want a safeguard. Is Hector listening to this?'

'You bet he is. Like what?'

'I'll tell you when we get to where we're going.'

Again there was a pause before he replied. 'You're a tricky bastard, Hardy.'

'Dealing with people like you I have to be.'

His short laugh was harsh. 'Okay, go north, cross the bridge over the channel and you'll see us. One hour.'

That made time tight. I collected a few things and told Marisha what was happening in bare outline. She took it in her stride.

'Ring Hector,' I said.

'Why?'

'Just do it. He's good at all this. Hasn't put a foot wrong so far.'

She tried.

'Nothing.'

I tried the number she'd given me for Templeton but there was no answer.

'Throwaway phones,' I said.

'As you expected.'

'Yeah. Templeton'd be able to organise cheap pay-as-you-go phones under false IDs. He'd have had the training.'

'But?'

'He will, I hope.'

Her hard shell seemed to crack. She put her arms around me and pressed close against me. 'You're not doing this for me, are you?'

I'd come this far and I wanted to see it through. I told her the truth—that I was doing it for me.

24

In the car I reached into my pocket for my keys and to check that I had my phone and found that Marisha had slipped a miniature tape recorder in there. Always working, Marisha. The phone rang.

'On the way, Hardy?'

'Yes.'

'Don't fuck up.'

I did as I was instructed, crossed the North Channel and saw a white SUV stopped at the side of the road. It was pulling a trailer carrying a Bobcat earth mover. I pulled up fifty metres behind it. Templeton stepped out just long enough for me to identify him and then the SUV, a Mitsubishi Triton, I now saw, moved off. Traffic was light and we edged at just a notch below the speed limit. I drew up close enough a couple of times to be sure there were three men in the car. The last thing I wanted to see was Clem with his bolt-cutters. But somehow I thought the delicacy of this operation would rule Clem out.

Following the Bobcat that swayed a bit on the trailer wasn't a comfortable feeling. I'm not particularly claustrophobic, but I didn't much like the idea of going down into a cave that had proved unstable and had to be dug out. It's not unusual when I faced unpleasant situations that something I've read pops into my mind. Driving along I recalled Henry Lawson's story 'His Father's Mate', in which a boy falls into a shaft when a windlass breaks. The story touched me when I read it as a schoolkid and the memory wasn't welcome now.

We passed Nelson Bay and other bijou Central Coast playgrounds and pushed north to a stretch where the road moved away from the coast. Templeton signalled and we turned off the highway down a secondary and through some heavy bush that was almost like rainforest. It couldn't have been far from the coast but it felt more like the Blue Mountains, with tall trees and outcrops of weathered rock. Well, Australia's like that, with patches of mini-climate and accompanying vegetation.

The paved road ended abruptly and poorly graded gravel took over. A sharp turn, which the Mitsubishi and trailer negotiated carefully, and we were on a bush track that only ran for a hundred metres before there was a gate.

Again, I pulled up short of the others. I thought of taking the .38 out of its compartment but changed my mind. I had another idea. I watched while Hector Tanner, looking not quite like himself out of his suit and in casual clothes, climbed down, glanced briefly back at me and opened the gate. A battered sign said PRIVATE PROPERTY KEEP OUT, but from the length of the grass on the track it didn't look as though anyone had been there in quite a while.

Through a break in the trees I saw what looked like an iron roof with afternoon sun glinting on it, but we swung off on a still rougher track and climbed a steep slope. We stopped where a clearing, which the bush was rapidly reclaiming, had been hacked out. I sat in the car and waited for them to come to me. I wanted to see exactly how they moved. You can tell a lot from that.

If he lacked his usual cocky strut, Twizell appeared undamaged. He busied himself with the chains holding down the Bobcat. Hector stood by ready to help. He watched as Templeton approached me and he seemed nervous, off-balance. Templeton came on with his long, easy stride, brimful of confidence. I got out of the car.

'Nice spot,' I said.

'It'll be nicer when two million bucks come into view.'

'You really think that'll happen?'

'It'll happen. Go and help with the Bobcat.'

I shrugged and went to the trailer. Twizell and I unclipped the chains while Tanner lowered the ramp. Twizell got up into the cabin, started the motor and inched the machine down the ramp onto the ground. I looked around but couldn't see anything that resembled a cave.

Twizell took notice of me for the first time. 'Thanks for this, Cliff. I knew I could count on you.'

'Let's get on with it,' Templeton said.

Twizell pointed to what appeared to be a high grassy mound at the edge of the clearing twenty metres away.

'Over there. It's been a few years and the place is overgrown. What happened was, the last five or so metres of the cave collapsed just as I got out. Dunno why. Just happened. We have to clear that, then we can get in.'

'How far in?' I said.

'Fair way.'

'Scared, Hardy?' Hector said.

I didn't answer. Templeton waved Twizell on and he moved the Bobcat into position and lowered the digging arm. The toothed bucket at the end of it tore into the grass-matted earth. We backed off as Twizell reversed, turned, swung the arm and dumped the load away to the side. He repeated the procedure again and again with the motor roaring, diesel fumes filling the air, and the loads varying from soft soggy stuff to sizeable chunks of rock.

'Hold it!' Templeton said as a load spilled out. He and I approached the pile that looked different from the others. Mixed in with the earth and rock were shreds of cloth and bones.

Twizell cut the motor and climbed down. 'That's him.'

'Bits of him,' Hector said. 'Sure you didn't kill him?'

'That'd be your style. No. I didn't. Poor bastard.'

Templeton snapped his fingers and Twizell went back to work. If other loads had bits of the skeleton, we didn't bother to look. I didn't see a skull. After a long, noisy, smelly time, Twizell had cleared the debris to reveal a gaping hole big enough for a large man to squeeze through. He cut the motor and wiggled his fingers in his ears.

'Should've had muffs. Hey, Hec, you've just been standing around. How about you get the torches and ropes?'

'Ropes?' I said.

'Have to go down a bit. Not too much. Don't worry. I'm an expert.'

I pointed to where a long bone stuck up. 'Yeah—an expert.'

'Fuck you,' Hector said. 'Get 'em yourself.'

'Do it,' Templeton said.

Hector swore, stumped back to the SUV and returned with two coiled ropes and two heavy torches. Twizell checked them. Even in the sunlight the beams were strong.

'Okay,' Templeton said, 'how long do you reckon?'

'Depends if there's water. This area must've copped some of the flood like everywhere else.'

'Shit,' I said.

'Shouldn't be too long; say three-quarters of an hour; but I'm not as fit as I was back when I first went in and it was dry. Could be a bit longer.'

Twizell wiped sweat from his face and smiled at Hector. 'What about the bags? No handles, Hec.'

Tanner swore again and moved off.

'You're enjoying this, Jack,' I said.

'In a funny way I am. Thought about it for long enough but I didn't see it quite like this. Still . . . I was sorry to hear about Kristie, Cliff.'

'Cut the crap,' Templeton said.

Tanner returned with two canvas backpacks which he dropped on the ground. He pulled a metal flask from his hip pocket and took a swig.

Twizell reached out. 'I could do with some of that.'

'Later,' Templeton snapped. 'Go!'

'No,' I said.

All three turned to look at me. Templeton pulled a pistol out from his jacket pocket. I pointed to it.

'That's what I mean. If you think Jack and I are going down into that hole and coming out with the money while you stand here with loaded guns you've got another think coming. No guns.'

'You took my fucking gun,' Hector said.

'Right, and I'm going to check there's none in your car and then Rod's going to lock his away in a compartment in my car with my gun. You'd need to tear the car apart to get at it.'

Templeton shrugged. 'Okay.'

'What d'you mean, okay?' Hector yelped. 'I thought you were running this show.'

'Hardy's got a point. No guns. Not needed.'

Hector muttered and took another swig from his flask. I looked through the Mitsubishi thoroughly and then

Templeton and I went to the Falcon and locked his Glock in the compartment. I put its key and the car key in my pocket. If Templeton was still working as a cop this was the moment to tell me but he said nothing. We walked back to where Hector and Twizell stood not talking.

'Put your backpack on under your jacket and do the jacket up,' Twizell said. 'You don't want anything sticking out or loose.'

He looped the coil of rope over his shoulder and I did the same. Hector turned away and pretended to be interested in the bone sticking out of the debris. Templeton nodded at us.

'Do it.'

Twizell scratched at his newly sprouted beard, stretched and worked his shoulders. He moved forward and turned sideways to get through the opening. He was much shorter than me but solidly built and it was a tight squeeze. I had to duck down but I got through easily enough. The smell inside the space was a mixture of foul, trapped air, damp rock and rotting vegetation.

I switched on my torch. 'We should have gas masks.'

'Been blocked a good while. There's air vents further down.'

'It's that "down" that worries me most,' I said, 'and air vents suggest water could get in.'

'I'll look after you. Hey, Cliff, that was a great move about that fucker's gun. You've got one tucked away somewhere, right?'

'Wrong.'

'Shit, I was counting on you.'

'Count again. Let's get on with it.'

25

My first problem, apart from the stink, was that I had to keep slightly hunched over, not a comfortable way to proceed. My favourite sport had been surfing, where the whole world is open to you. Even boxing, although you're in a confined space for the contest, takes place in a bigger space. The idea of enjoying creeping along in an underground alley in a half-light was alien to me. But the secret of getting things done is to do them and not waste energy complaining.

I followed Twizell, who, I had to admit, showed some talent in the caper—signalling me to warn of hazards like jutting-out rocks and unevenness underfoot. The air quality improved but what I'd suspected proved to be true. Water had got in when the area was flooded and we were slogging through ankle-deep mud and splashing through puddles. After what felt like half an hour, but was probably less, of steady but gradual descending we came to the first drop. We

229

needed to get down to a level about ten metres below where we were. Water dripped over the edge.

Twizell shone his torch beam around, located a solid anchor point and tied his rope around it.

'Get down backwards, using the rope, and sort of walk down the face,' he said, 'like this.'

He disappeared over the edge and I heard a few grunts and then he shone his torch up at me.

'It's easy,' he said.

It wasn't. I was stiffer than was right for the job; my palms were sweaty and the rope slipped and burned them and I bumped my knee several times on the way down.

'Told you,' he said. 'Picked this because I knew I could get in and out easily.'

I grunted and rubbed my hands together.

'Sorry, should have got gloves for you.'

'I'll be all right. Let's go.'

'Notice it's a bit warmer?'

'Yeah.'

'Further you go down the warmer it gets. I've been in some caves hot as—'

'Jack, we haven't got all day.'

The ground was very rough now and Twizell stumbled a few times and swore. But it was drier. He was less cavalier with his torch after that and kept it trained a metre or so in front of him.

'At least it's dry,' I said.

'So far. All depends on the fucking vents and the flood.' His laugh was almost a giggle. 'Money might've floated away. Wouldn't that be a hoot?'

'You used to do this for fun?'

'Yeah. I'll do it again if I get through this. Reckon we will?'

'Fair chance.'

The cave, which after the drop had been high enough for me to stand and wide enough for easy passage, suddenly turned a corner and narrowed. Twizell moved cautiously and I heard a sigh of relief from him.

'What?'

'It's okay. There was a bit of a collapse here first time and I wondered, but it seems all right now.' He sounded nervous and as if talking helped. 'Tell you one place I wouldn't do it.'

I didn't want him nervous. 'Where's that?'

'Fucking New Zealand. Imagine being down here when—'

'Shut up!'

'Getting edgy?'

'You were.'

'All right, we're nearly there. Here's the next drop. Much the same.'

'Any water?'

He shone his torch. 'Looks all right.'

He went through the same procedure and dropped over the edge. I got out my Swiss army knife, hacked two chunks out of my denim shirt, wrapped them around my hands and went down the rope. The drop was nearly twice as long as the first but I was more careful and got down more slowly but without damage. Twizell studied me as I stuffed the cloth in my pocket.

'You're doing okay.'

A childish reaction, but I enjoyed his praise—momentarily.

'The money. Where?'

'Over here.'

He took two paces and our torch beams focused on a ledge in the rock wall. Eight bundles, sealed in heavy plastic, each about the size of a six-pack of beer, but without handy finger holes, sat on the ledge.

Twizell's laugh was almost hysterical. 'Here we are, mate. Not protected by snakes or skulls or anything. Just beautiful, beautiful money.'

I'd had charge of large amounts of money myself, and bodyguarded people carrying still larger amounts, but this was the most I'd ever seen in one chunk. It looked oddly innocent and it was in itself, but it was associated with a lot of things that were anything but innocent. My problem was its future associations. I thought this while taking off my jacket and unstrapping the backpack.

'It's just money,' I said. 'Here today and gone tomorrow. Load it up and let's get out of this fucking hole.'

We loaded the plastic blocks into the backpacks, four each. Bulky, but not heavy. Then we retraced our steps. Twizell went up the rope at the second drop like a cat up a tree. I struggled; the backpack made me awkward and my hands hurt despite the wrappings. I made it with Twizell's help.

The downward slope hadn't felt very severe, but now it was upward and it seemed steep in spots. I had to stop for a rest a couple of times. I needed to catch my breath and the confinement and smell were getting to me.

'How did they treat you?' I asked on the second pause.

'How d'you mean?'

'Didn't rough you up?'

'Hec wanted to but bloody Rod wouldn't let him.'

'Were you worried about the bolt-cutters?'

Twizell had plenty of wind. He laughed. 'That bloke got picked up by the cops. Warrants out on him, apparently. I wasn't sorry to hear that. You right now?'

'Just about. I'm wondering if Templeton has really gone over to the other side. Do you reckon he could still be the undercover cop playing along with Hector to . . . ?'

Twizell shook his head, gestured, and his torch beam zoomed around the space. 'No way. He's in it with him a hundred per cent. Were you banking on that to get us out of this in one piece?'

'Not exactly.'

'That really fills me with confidence. Come on, we've still got that other rope to get up and we're well past the time I said. They'll be getting edgy.'

Despite giving me the hurry-up, Twizell slowed down

from that point. He bumped against a projecting rock and swore as blood spread over his neck and dripped down into his collar. He stopped to mop it with the sleeve of his jacket. I shone my torch and saw where the wound caused by the end of Templeton's sawn-off had been reopened.

I thought: *Where's that shotgun?*

We reached the second rope and I stopped Twizell before he took his grip. 'The shottie, where is it?'

'I dunno. You looked in the SUV, didn't you?'

'Yeah. You sure he didn't stick it under the seat in the Bobcat or something like that?'

'I'm not sure. Shit, you're putting the wind up me.'

'Probably nothing. He seems pretty confident he can bring this off peacefully.'

'Are you?'

'No. Let's get up this bloody rope.'

Twizell was much less nimble this time. He stood at the top with the rope in his grasp as I moved to grab it. His torch beam blinded me.

'What're you doing?' I said.

His voice seemed to come from far away and there was a slight echo to it. 'Thinking.'

'About what?'

'Leaving you here and negotiating. You'll never get up that rock face.'

That made me wonder about Twizell and the backpacker but it was no time for wondering.

'Forget it, Jack. Half the money's with me. They'd send you down for it or Templeton'd come after it himself and I'm in no state to fight him. He'd leave me here and you'd have done your last cave for sure. The odds are in favour of not upsetting them. I don't like it any more than you do, but . . .'

The beam flicked away.

'Yeah, yeah. Come up. You can't live forever, right?'

It wasn't what I wanted to hear, but he let go of the rope and I went up more easily than I'd thought I could. We stood together looking down the narrow, lower and wet rest of the way out.

'When you're caving,' Twizell said, 'you have options— left or right, up or down, go on or go back. You know?'

'Yeah, like in life, but not right now.'

We went on; I crouched where I had to and ploughed through the mud towards the clean air and the light.

26

Twizell propped at the entrance and I had to push him to get out. I hadn't expected anything good, but I hadn't anticipated anything like what I saw when I lurched through into the light. Three men in tracksuits wearing balaclavas and carrying pistols stood about twenty metres away. Hector and Templeton were on their knees in front of them with their hands behind their heads.

The one in the middle gestured with his pistol. 'Come on out, boys, and join the party. Have to say you don't look so good.'

Twizell and I were wet and muddied to our knees. We moved forward.

'Take off the backpacks and put them on the ground.'

'Who the fuck are you?' Twizell said.

'All in good time. Do it.'

We did it. He waved one of his companions, who, unlike

237

the others, was wearing gloves, forward. He put his pistol on the ground, knelt and undid the Velcro fasteners and lifted out a block from each of the backpacks. Then he shoved them back in.

'Good,' the one who was doing the talking said. The third man, a big guy, handed his gun to the one who'd opened the backpacks, lifted both bags by their straps and walked away. I tracked him as he moved past the Bobcat and the SUV. The Mitsubishi sagged to one side on slashed tyres.

Templeton let his hands drop but he didn't stand up. The spokesman barked an order which Templeton ignored. 'Don't you get it, Jack? They're the ones who lifted the money in the first place.'

'Shit,' Twizell said.

'That's not very eloquent,' the leader said, 'but that's right. That's who we are. You caused us a lot of trouble.'

'How did you know Twizell had moved the money?' I said.

The leader laughed and his gun didn't move a fraction. 'Johnnie here got on the gunja when he was inside and told someone what he should have kept to himself. Just once, but we heard about it.'

'Fuck,' Twizell said. 'How did you track us here?'

'We've kept tabs on you from the minute you got out.'

'The helicopter,' I said.

'Right, and bugs in certain cars.'

Templeton started to rise. 'Who cares?' He looked challengingly at me, inviting me to make a move, risk casualties, upset the controlled scene. The other man moved quickly; he kicked the back of Templeton's right knee, collapsing him.

'Bad idea,' the leader said, 'but marks for guts.'

He lowered his pistol and shot Hector in the back of the neck, Chinese execution style.

Twizell yelped. Hector twitched twice and lay still. Twizell threw up. I shut my eyes for a split second then turned to look at the shooter. He'd lost interest and shook his head at Templeton and me.

'Just him. Old score settled,' he said. 'You lot keep cool and you'll be all right. Now, my friend with the money's got a rifle with a scope in his hands by now and he can hit your left or right ball at this distance. Stay cool and we're out of here and no one gets hurt.'

I looked down at Hector.

'He was nothing,' the leader said.

The two of them put their pistols away and spread out as they backed off to give the guy with the rifle a clear field of fire. Templeton got to his feet. There was a sharp report and a bullet clipped the trees just above where we stood. A motor started. Birds flew up at the noise and then there was silence.

'Have to admire that,' Templeton said.

Twizell looked ready to hit him. 'Admire it? They've got the fucking money.'

Templeton examined Hector's body. 'It's your fault, getting stoned and blabbing.'

'I don't remember it.'

'Very stoned.' Templeton walked to the SUV.

'What's he doing?' Twizell said. 'That thing's out of action.'

Templeton rummaged in the glove box of the car and came up with a pair of handcuffs. He strode back, jerked Hector's splayed arms behind his back and cuffed him.

'What're you doing?' Twizell yelped.

Templeton looked at me. 'I was just doing my job, drawing Hector out of hiding. I was all set to hand him and the money over when these three appeared. Right, Hardy?'

I shrugged. 'Difficult to say.'

'You lying bastard,' Twizell said. 'You were in it for the money. I've got it—you did a deal with those cunts. This was all staged.'

'Why would I do that, Jack?'

Twizell was practically hopping from foot to foot in his agitation. 'You probably knew that they'd heard a whisper and that they'd come after the money one way or another. This way you get a cut and don't have to worry about them.'

'What d'you think, Hardy?'

I shrugged. 'It's a theory.'

'That's all it is.'

Templeton smiled but I couldn't tell whether it was the smile of someone who'd got away with something or whether he was just amused. He was a hard man to read at the best of times and this wasn't one of those. He took his mobile from his pocket. 'Prove it,' he said.

27

Templeton seemed to have his mojo back as an undercover operator, if he'd ever lost it. He worked his mobile, using the codes, delivering punchy messages. Twizell and I sat on the edge of the trailer and watched him.

'I wouldn't mind a slug of Hector's vodka,' Twizell said. 'Reckon he'd let me?'

'He wouldn't. He has to control the crime scene.'

'He'll have to control more than that. He's lying.'

'Look, I found out a bit about him. He's seen as a bit of a loose cannon by the police but apparently he's done some pretty good work. They'll go along with him on this. They're no worse off in terms of the money and they won't be grieving over Hector.'

'No one will. So what're you saying?'

'Just that I'm not going to say any more than I have to. If

Templeton's version's accepted by the cops I'm not going to contradict it. I'm finished with all this.'

He scratched his beard and checked that he wasn't bleeding from the neck wound. He was quiet for a while, as if reviewing everything that had happened.

'Hey, what about the old papers and the professor and that?'

'They were in the car with him and Kristie. Gone. Wakefield said it was the stuff he was after but that's all he said. We'll never know.'

'Great. I hate to see this bastard get away with everything.'

'He hasn't. If he was really after the money then he's lost out. And I think he had genuine feelings for Kristie, so he's lost out there, too.'

'Yeah, poor thing; she had no luck. I've still got some problems. I've broken parole by not reporting and—' he waved his hand at the cave opening, 'doing all this.'

'Templeton has to say you were under duress. You'll be all right as long as you stay on the right side of him.'

He nodded. 'Hate to do it, but.'

Sirens wailed, coming closer. I stood up. 'He's a risk-taker. He'll get out of this probably, but he'll come to grief sooner or later.'

'You believe that?'

'I don't believe anything much, but I've seen it happen before.'

Within minutes, the clearing was full of vehicles—police

cars marked and unmarked and an ambulance, and people—uniforms, detectives, SOC types. Templeton talked, pointed, demonstrated. Twizell and I were like minor actors in a movie—waiting to play our bit parts.

28

It seemed to work out pretty much as Templeton had orchestrated it. I cooperated to the extent of helping him to recover his gun. Undercover police were given very wide terms of reference and Templeton hadn't done anything too far outside the boundaries. Whether they believed he'd handcuffed Hector before he'd been executed I didn't know, but they had two leading crime figures dead and one up on serious charges and were satisfied.

When Roderick Fitzjames Templeton climbed into a police car and left the clearing outside the cave, that was the last I saw of him. I knew that, if the police bought his story, they'd protect him. They'd try not to use him as a witness against Joseph and, if they had to, they'd disguise him and give him a code name. W3 or some such. And then he'd disappear into the netherworld of undercover work. Or perhaps Jack Twizell's theory was correct, and

Templeton would just bide his time until he retired in comfort.

Twizell's parole was withdrawn. He faced charges of associating with criminals and was under investigation for his involvement in the death of Roy Flanagan. DNA analysis had confirmed the identity of the British backpacker. However, the state of his remains prevented any clear conclusion as to how he'd been killed and the investigation lapsed. So did the criminal association charge.

It turned out that he'd had a nest egg tucked away that had financed him into a lease on his SUV and a short-term rental at the serviced apartments. He got the car back, paid the long-term parking fine I'd landed him with, and was soon driving around Newcastle looking for opportunities.

Marisha came to Sydney to talk to her publisher and agent. We met up and spent a day and a night together. Inevitably, we talked a lot about what had happened.

'Your friend Jack Twizell tried to tap me for money in return for information about what he called the showdown.'

'That sounds right,' I said. 'What did you say?'

'I told him to get lost. He's a spiv, but you can't help liking him a bit. I told him I'd got all the info I needed on that from you, which wasn't quite true.'

'How d'you mean?'

'You didn't use the bloody tape recorder.'

I laughed. 'The truth is I forgot about it, but it was no

time with all those guns around for putting hands in pockets and fumbling for switches.'

She went back to Newcastle and I took care of business. I got an email from Marisha telling me she'd applied for a job in Sydney and was hopeful. I wasn't sure how things would go if she got it, but there were worse ways to spend time than with Marisha Henderson, author of *The Tanners: Crime and family in Newcastle*.

I opened a file on the case and called it simply 'Dunbar'. After a visit to Megan and Ben I walked through St Stephen's cemetery again and looked at the monument, thinking that the wreck had claimed a few more victims.

Thanks to Jean Bedford for everything. Thanks to Michael Wilding for alerting me to Henry Kendall's poem and to the Reserve Bank officer who told me what two million dollars in $100 notes would look like in bulk.